КОММЕНТАТОРА

ОЕВОЙ ВАНГАРД

В СЕРДЕЧНОЙ ОБСТАНОВКЕ

ПРОДОЛЖЕНИЕ АГРЕССИИ

Нападение американо-сайгонских войск на Камбоджу ◆ Заявление вице-президента США ◆ Усиливаются протесты против грязной войны ◆ Отмежеваться от курса Вашингтона — призывают английские профсоюзы ◆ правительство Великобритании

ПНОМПЕНЬ, 5. (ТАСС). Американские совер...

НЬЮ-ЙОРК, 5. (ТАСС). Перед глав...

БАНГКОК, 5. (ТАСС). Вице-пре...

ЛОНДОН, 5. (ТАСС). В связи с...

НЬЮ-ЙОРК, 5. (ТАСС). Война, ко...

ДЕЛИ, 5. (ТАСС). И...

Из потока сообщений

Культурное сотрудничество развивается

Несмотря на заявления президента Никсона

Иностранные кампании — под государственный контроль

ПРИМЕРТЫ И СТЕНЕ

САЙГОН, 5. (Франс Пресс).

Международный

О. С...

ЕСТЬ 400 КИЛОМЕТР

Eastern European Poets Series #45

ДАРЫ СОЛНЦА

Репортаж с цитрусовой плантации

Г. КАЛАНДАР...
Колхоз имени Ленина
Таджикской ССР.

СРЕДИ КНИГ

С ЛЮБОВЬЮ К ЛЮДЯМ

В. ПОЛТОРАЦКИЙ.

ЭКСПЕРИМЕНТ

Возвращаясь к напечатанному

КОЛХОЗНИКИ ОДОБРИЛИ

ТАДЖИКУРГАН, 5. (Корр. «Правды» Т. Жануляков).

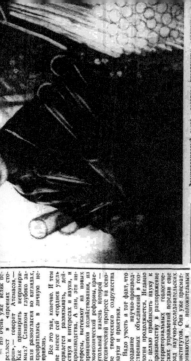

Dmitri Alexandrovich Prigov

SOVIET TEXTS

Translated from Russian by Simon Schuchat with Ainsley Morse

SOVIET TEXTS

Dmitri Alexandrovich Prigov

© Novoe Literaturnoe Obozrenie, Moscow, 2020

Translation © Simon Schuchat, 2020

Introduction and notes on the poems © Simon Schuchat, 2020

Eastern European Poets Series #45

ISBN 978-1-946433-07-7

First Edition, First Printing, 2020

Ugly Duckling Presse

The Old American Can Factory

232 Third Street, #E-303

Brooklyn, NY 11215

uglyducklingpresse.org

Distributed by SPD/Small Press Distribution (US), by Inpress Books (UK),
and by Coach House Books (Canada) via Publishers Group Canada.

Cover by Jamie's PEN&INK

Design and typesetting by Jamie's PEN&INK and Don't Look Now!

The type is Garamond, Helvetica CY, and Russo One

Books printed offset and bound at McNaughton & Gunn

Covers printed offset by Prestige Printing on Mohawk Via Felt 100% PC Cool White

The publication of this book was made possible, in part, by a grant from the Mikhail Prokhorov
Foundation TRANSCRIPT Programme to Support Translations of Russian Literature, and
by the continued support of the New York State Council on the Arts.

Table of Contents

Translator's Note

We usually think of Russian dissident literature as serious and heavy and full of the suffering of the gulag and the struggle of the individual conscience against the oppression of the state. However, as Stalinism turned into Khrushchev's "Thaw" and then Brezhnev's "Stagnation," Soviet underground and oppositional culture experienced a crucial shift. Some dissident writers, like Joseph Brodsky and his somewhat bohemian circle, simply tried to ignore the state and history ("that wolf," as Osip Mandelstam would call it). One could say the same of some of the abstract and expressionist painters (the Lianozovo school and others), who went on about their work outside of the official art institutions, hoping not to be noticed. But for some artists and writers, this form of "peaceful coexistence" was not enough, and they started to make work that poked fun at the Soviet version of reality quite directly, and in a variety of genres and media. Among them was Dmitri Alexandrovich Prigov—a founding figure of what came to be called Moscow Conceptualism.

Dmitri Alexandrovich Prigov was born in Moscow in 1940 and was trained as a sculptor at the Stroganov Art Institutue in Moscow. Almost until the collapse of the Soviet Union, his writing circulated solely in samizdat, or in overseas publications. An inventive and prolific writer in all genres, Prigov was something like a Pop artist in a land without consumer culture. His writing is a part of, and even central to, the broader world of "nonconformist," "SotsArt," and conceptualist art scenes of late Soviet "really existing Socialism." His visual artist contemporaries included Komar and Melamid, Ilya Kabakov, and Erik Bulatov, all of whom emigrated (or were exiled) from the USSR in the 1970s and 1980s. Trained as a sculptor, and working in a milieu that was populated as much by visual artists as by poets, Prigov produced a vast oeuvre of graphic works and found and altered objects, in addition to countless poems, visual texts, and prose works. He appeared in Pavel Lungin's Cannes-award-winning late-Soviet film *Taxi Blues*. He even worked as a municipal architect, though one is hard-pressed to know what he did in that occupation. He also frequently took part in performance art events with the Moscow Collective Actions group, and in collaborative performances with others in the "unofficial" art scene, such as sculptor Grisha Bruskin, poet Lev Rubinstein, and experimental jazz drummer Vladimir Tarasov. In 1986, he was arrested for wheat-pasting and distributing leaflets of poems addressed to his fellow "citizens," and was briefly detained in a psychiatric hospital—disciplinary psychiatry was a common Soviet technique for dealing with dissidents: clearly anyone who went up against the norms of the Soviet State must have been crazy. He was released after protests from establishment literary figures.

After the collapse of the Soviet Union in 1991, Prigov's text production continued without interruption, even as he broadened his practice as an artist, creating art installations, video, performance, and music. He published widely at home and received awards, among them the Pushkin Prize of the Alfred Toepfer Foundation in 1993, and the Boris Pasternak Prize in 2002. He traveled extensively, visiting the United States, Western Europe, and former East Bloc countries and Soviet republics, exhibiting his visual work and giving readings and performances, and interacting with his peers in the international avant-garde. His travels to Japan resulted in a novel, *Just My Japan*. He returned to the screen with a small role in *Khrustalyov, My Car!*, Aleksei German's 1998 film about Stalin's death.

In the post-Soviet era, though he was free to publish, exhibit, perform, and travel, Prigov's oppositional stance did not bend. He encouraged and inspired the next generation of conceptual dissident artists, such as the well-known Voina (War) group and, later, Pussy Riot, who dedicated their intervention at the 2018 World Cup in Moscow to Prigov's memory.

Prigov died in Moscow in 2007 at the age of 66; a lifespan longer than average for a Russian male of his generation. En route to a performance with the Voina group—for which he planned to read poems inside a wardrobe while being carried up the stairs of Moscow University—he collapsed in the subway after a heart attack.

§

At times, Prigov claimed that he planned to write 42,000 texts, although he also said this would take him 4,000 years. By some accounts, he claimed to have completed 24,000 or 36,000 poems. The exact number is hard to verify, but behind this mythology is a serious point: the sheer quantity (not to mention the variety) was a work in itself, and by being so prolific—a kind of Stakhanovite shock worker exceeding the demanded industrial quota—Prigov redefined the role of the poet away from the Romantic identity inhabited by poets like Brodsky.

In the present edition, we can only fit a sample of Prigov's overall literary oeuvre. His "incomplete" collected works fill five thick volumes. However, our selection does include many of his key works, including the Soviet-era writings that made his reputation and which the interested Russian reader would likely know, as well as some of his most innovative and powerful post-Soviet works.

Prigov's earliest works in this collection dismantle Soviet ritual linguistic practice. For example, in "Description of Objects" Prigov adapts the rigid jargon of dialectical materialism to descriptions of symbolically charged objects, producing a new Soviet encyclopedia where everything is almost the same as everything else. In "Obituaries," the great figures of Russian literature are memorialized with the canned formulas of the Soviet press.

The poetic sequences of the seventies and eighties, such as "Apotheosis of the Offissa" or "The Image of Reagan in Soviet Literature," show the sometimes maddening and generally ridiculous world of everyday life in the time of the super power's decline. His stories from the same era give us Soviet and Russian history and especially literary history as no doubt the majority of day-dreaming Soviet middle school students knew it, albeit even more muddled, debased, and absurd.

Of the many strands of Prigov's post-Soviet writing, we have included pieces where he is almost scientific, as he recalculates time, enumerates causation, equalizes brain power, and inventories death and the figures and motifs of life. Some of these poems are comprehensive catalogs, while others, in true conceptualist fashion, take a proposition and work it through to its ultimate demise.

While Prigov's writing is very definitely of the Soviet and post-Soviet world, it is also fully equal to, and sometimes consonant with contemporaneous avant-garde writing elsewhere in the world. Many of his conceptual works bring to mind the French writer Georges Perec (although Prigov's use of mathematics is entirely unlike that of the Oulipo group). I hear echoes of Jack Spicer in Prigov's serial sequences, such as "Moscow and the Muscovites," as themes weave in and out to create a fragmentary, implied narrative. His stories of Soviet-Russian mythology, such as "Awesome Stone Avenger" or "The Delegate from Vasilevsky Island" recall the wistful beauty of Bill Hutton's *History of America*: both are equal panoramas of mingled misremembered fact and error, befitting the true past of a Superpower. Throughout, there is an over-the-top tone, and a feel of sheer fun in writing, which might remind an American reader of Ron Padgett and Ted Berrigan's collaborative *Bean Spasms*.

In the manner of Stalin's praise for Mayakovsky, we might say: Dmitri Alexandrovich Prigov was a leading writer of the late Soviet and early post-Soviet era; his contribution to world letters is of great significance and should be better recognized; indifference to his memory, if not a crime, is at the very least a grave error. My hope is that this collection may play a part in correcting that error.

Acknowledgments

I am especially grateful to Matvei Yankelevich and the rest of the Ugly Duckling Presse collective for their confidence in this project and its translator. I owe a special debt of gratitude to Ainsley Morse who steered me away from all sorts of mistakes. Mark Lipovetsky, editor of Prigov's collected works for Novoe Literaturnoe Obozrenie, provided guidance at an early stage, and generously gave his advice throughout the process. For helping me enter the world of matters Russian and guiding me once there, I want to thank several ambassadors: Lynn Pascoe, Don Keyser, Jim Collins, John Ordway, Sandy Vershbow, Toria Nuland, Cliff Bond, Mary Warlick and, most of all, Steve Young. I first studied Russian at the Foreign Service Institute under Emily Yurevich and her colleagues, without whom, assuredly, I would never have read Prigov in the first place. On the literary front Charles Bernstein, Bob Rosenthal, Bob Holman, Judith Hall, Maureen Owen, and Alice Notley provided various forms of encouragement and assistance, as did, in the realm of specifically Russian literary translation, Peter Tegel and John Glad. Finally, thanks to Christine Chen for everything. All errors and misunderstandings are mine and should not be blamed on any of the above, or anyone else for that matter.

I am obliged to note that the State Department, which had posted me in Moscow in the 1990s, has reviewed this translation and posed no objection to its publication. The opinions and characterizations in these pieces are those of the author, and do not represent official positions of the United States Government.

Pieces in this collection, in earlier versions, have been published in *Skanky Possum, Talisman, The Literary Review, The Recluse,* and *The Antioch Review.* I am grateful to the editors of these publications.

— *Simon Schuchat, August 2019*

ЖИЗНЕННАЯ СИЛА ЛЕНИНИЗМА

ПОСЛЕ КРИТИКИ

◆ ПОМОЩЬ СЕЛЬСКИМ СТРОЙКАМ

◆ ПРИУСАДЕБНЫЙ УЧАСТОК ВОЗВРАЩЕН

◆ НАКАЗАНИЕ ПО ЗАСЛУГАМ

О. ЧЕРНИКОВ,
Директор союза
«Избыльненское».

Д. АКУЛЬШ
(Корр. «Пра

беседы, семинары, конференции

КИЕВ, 5. (Корр. «Правды»).

ЮНОШИ И ДЕВУШКИ— на трактор

КРАСНОДАР, 5.

SOVIET TEXTS

Высокая награда

ПОЧЕМУ ВЕД... СТРОКОЙ ПИСЬ...

UNDER ME

(1994)

Advisory Note

Didn't a lot happen in my reign, under me? Any less than happened under anyone else? But this particular specific "I" represents a universal, operational point enumerating where specific coordinates intersect. Or rather, truly, to give oneself over entirely to it, one has already oriented oneself to arbitrary comparisons and contrasts: an assembly table, from across which will seep past a procession of details, elements, events, which took place "under me," gathering together into a universal mechanism of the cosmos that makes sense to me, combining in one system all the sounds, signs, names, and tears, while delegating emptiness as though remaining in life to carry their own functioning beyond the limits of their functioning, dragging toward me (that is, to themselves) all that is rather distant, and, through the inertia of all of their pivotal varying sites, declare the possibility of a privatization procedure of the much, much more distant past as well, and which, on appeal, allow for the adding on of an entirely possible future.

Basically, to say it straight, everything was, happened, and took place under me.

Stalin, Khrushchev, Brezhnev died under me
And Georgi Dimitrov, Vilko Chervenkov also died under me
And Klement Gottwald, Antonin Zápotocký, Gustáv Husák, and
    Ludvík Svoboda died under me
And under me Bolesław Bierut died
And under me Josip Broz Tito died
And Enver Hoxha died under me
Under me Wilhelm Pieck, Otto Grotewohl,
Walter Ulbricht, and Erich Honecker died
Mao Zedong, Zhou Enlai, Lin Biao died under me
And de Gaulle died under me
And Adenauer, Brandt, Schmidt, Strauss died
Churchill and Eden died under me
Roosevelt and Truman died under me
Under me Paasikivi and Urho Kekkonen died
Palmiro Togliatti and Luigi Longo died under me
Franco and Salazar died under me
And Hirohito died under me
And many, many, many others
Also died under me

Under me Mosaddegh, Lumumba, and Allende were killed
Zia-ul-Haq, both Gandhis, Somoza
The President of Bangladesh, I don't remember his name, were killed
The Prime Minister of Korea and all his cabinet were killed,
Yes, and Kennedy, Kennedy, and Kennedy were killed under me
Sadat, Ceauşescu and Rabin were killed

Who else?
Olof Palme was killed
Aldo Moro killed
And many, many, many others were also killed
Under me

There were wars under me
Egypt with England and France
North Korea with the South
War between India and Pakistan
War between India and China
China and Vietnam had a war
And, of course, yes! I completely forgot, the Second World Great
    Patriotic was also under me
England and Argentina had a war under me
And Israel with Egypt
And Greece had a war with Turkey under me
And under me there was war between Iraq and Iran
And Iraq and Kuwait
And Ethiopia and Somalia
And the USSR and Afghanistan
And Peru with Honduras
And Zambia with Zaire, I guess,
And others, and others, and the others
All these wars were under me

The British Empire ended under me
Yes, under me
The French Empire ended under me
Rhodesia was declared and South Africa ended
Under me Yugoslavia ended and fell apart
And what's even sadder—the USSR ended under me
And Great India ended under me
And the German Democratic Republic, the GDR, ended under me
But a unified Germany appeared under me
And a unified Korea separated under me

And the United Arab Republic was declared and also dissolved in
    my time
The Warsaw Pact was dissolved under me
And of course, Czechoslovakia divided into the Czech Republic and
    Slovakia under me
So, many, many of these different entities
Were formed and then, or a little later,
Or in their own time
Fell apart under me

Under me Pasternak, Akhmatova, Zabolotsky, Kharms, Vvedensky
    and Tatlin passed away
Picasso, Matisse, Camus, Sartre, Dalí and Duchamp passed away
    under me
And Eliot, Pound, Frost, Borges
And Fellini passed away under me
And Shostakovich passed away under me
And Prokofiev passed away under me
And Dunayevsky passed away under me
And Stravinsky passed away under me
And Cage passed away under me
Nureyev, Callas, Corbusier, Lysenko, Fadeyev, Sholokhov, Gagarin,
    Orwell, and Monroe
And many, many, many many many marvelous people
Passed away under me

Under me Rubinstein, Sorokin, Kabakov, Schnittke, and Tarkovsky
    made their appearance
And Stallone, Schwarznegger, Kim Basinger, Michael Jackson
    appeared under me
Tarantino, Platini, van Basten, Wim Wenders also appeared under me
Jeff Koons appeared under me, too
And Ciccolina appeared under me
And Ravi Shankar appeared under me
Mike Tyson, Schumacher, Agassi, Magic Johnson appeared under me,
    too

Under me Chikatilo, Thompson, Carlos Ilich, Basayev, and Che
   Guevara appeared
Gagarin appeared under me, too
Yes, and the Beatles, the Beatles, the Beatles, all four appeared under me
And Salman Rushdie appeared under me
And Derrida appeared under me
And many, many many others, not remembered here
Appeared under me

Under me it was declared that a person is not a person,
But a collection of all sorts of genes, that's what was declared under me
Under me it was discovered that existence is possible in outer space
And that existence is possible under the earth was discovered under me
And all kinds of computers and robots were discovered under me
And AIDS was discovered under me
And the air, full of flying saucers, was discovered under me
And all sorts of peculiarities pertaining to the waters, mountains,
   plants, and animals
All this was discovered under me
Also, I forgot, the atom bomb was discovered under me
And aircraft carriers, rockets, lasers, bullets with hollow centers were
   discovered under me
And that the ancients were right in many respects was discovered
   under me

But meanwhile a great multitude, a multitude, a multitude of all sorts
   of nonsense
Was also, once again, discovered under me

But horror, fear, and madness
Were discovered under me with a new, mad force
Ignorance and terror were declared under me
And under me passions were declared with hitherto unknown force
And under me despair was declared with a force hitherto unknown in
   this world
But joy and the anticipation of joy

Also appeared under me with force hitherto unknown in this long-
    suffering world
Compassion also appeared under me
With an undisguised force hitherto unknown in this long-suffering
    world
And struggles and betrayal and weakness and the overcoming of
    weakness
Appeared under me like instantaneous flashes of an undisguised force
    hitherto unknown in this long-suffering world
And finally, unknown and indescribable things
Appeared under me like instantaneous and intoxicating flashes of an
    undisguised force hitherto unknown in this long-suffering world

Under me practically everything was unavoidable
And under me my parents were, practically, unavoidable
And I was, practically, unavoidable under me
My sister was practically unavoidable under me
And chicken pox, jaundice, scarlet fever, diphtheria, measles, mumps,
    and polio were, practically unavoidable under me
And socialism, under me, was practically unavoidable
And capitalism, under me, was practically unavoidable
And, under me, colonialism, imperialism, communism,
    expansionism, behaviorism, and existentialism were practically
    unavoidable
But on the other hand, rising homosexuality, and conceptualism,
    feminism and environmentalism, terrorism and synergism were
    practically unavoidable under me
Under me the earth, sky, fields, woods, meadows, hills, streams,
    earthquakes, floods, fires, crashes, temptations, dangers,
    revelations, changes, solaces, purifications, annihilations,
    takeovers, disappearances, and everything, everything,
    everything,
Was practically unavoidable under me

DESCRIPTION
OF OBJECTS

(1979)

Advisory Note

The objective of this collection was to give an accurate description of objects, in a recognizable portrait, as well as demystify them, bringing to bear all of humankind's centuries-old socio-cultural and spiritual experience, along with the latest scientific data.

In our choice of objects we were guided by the principle of their greatest significance and their prevalence in man's social, labor, and everyday activities. The system and methodology for description that we have developed will, with time, allow us to continue our efforts and ultimately provide a complete inventory of the world that surrounds us.

Egg

Comrades! The egg is one of the most prevalent objects in man's social, labor, and everyday activities.

It consists of a complex curved continuous surface with complex organic contents. In size it ranges from 20 mm to infinity in length.

It is depicted by joining two palms, each folded to form a hemisphere.

In daily life it is used as feed for all types of livestock and humans in raw form, in the form of fried eggs, omelettes, boiled, and so on.

The historical origins of the egg are associated with the appearance on earth of egg-laying animals, which is inaccurate, since eggs of natural origin can be found much earlier.

The image of the egg is often used as a spiritual and mystical symbol of the original cosmological substance, which is absolutely inaccurate from a scientific point of view, since it would be more correct to consider the idea of the origin of the world as the creative act of a demiurge over the course of seven days.

Sometimes the image of the egg is associated with that of social class as a sort of substance and with a rigid form of class ideology, which is inaccurate from the Marxist point of view, since the mechanism of interaction between class and ideology is fundamentally different.

Because of the difficulty of achieving the curved continuous surface and the delicacy of the shell, this object is virtually impossible to reproduce. For the reasons indicated above, its actual existence is considered unlikely.

Cross

Comrades! The cross is one of the most prevalent objects in man's social, labor, and everyday activities.

It consists of an intersection of two absolutely perpendicular narrow planes. In size it ranges from 20 mm to infinity in length.

It is depicted by the perpendicular overlapping of two fingers of different hands.

In daily life it is used for crucifixion, for wearing around the neck, as a support on buildings used for religious purposes, for hanging clothes to dry, to fix coordinates, and so on.

The historical origins of the cross are associated with the appearance of legal institutions and crime prevention practices in ancient Rome, which is inaccurate, since much earlier crosses of natural origin have been found.

The image of the cross is often used as a spiritual and mystical symbol of the world tree, which is absolutely inaccurate from a scientific point of view, since it would be more correct to consider a pillar to be a symbol of the world tree.

Sometimes the image of the cross is associated with that of the intersection of the individual will and the will of the state, which is inaccurate from a Marxist point of view, since the mechanism of interaction between the individual and the state is fundamentally different.

Because of the complexity of achieving an absolutely perpendicular intersection of the two planes, this object is virtually impossible to reproduce. For the reasons indicated above, its actual existence is considered unlikely.

Pillow

Comrades! The pillow is one of the most prevalent objects in man's social, labor, and everyday activities.

It consists of two pieces of material sewn together with an internal filling in compliance with a precise balance between elasticity and firmness. In size it ranges from 20 mm to infinity in length.

It is depicted by pressing two hands together, palms facing inward.

In daily life it is used to place under the head, elbow, the ribs, at the back, under the buttocks, and so on.

The historical origins of the pillow are associated with the moment of class stratification in primitive society, which is inaccurate, since much earlier pillows of natural origin have been found.

The image of the pillow has often been used as a spiritual and mystical symbol of female sexual energy, the female sexual organs or the womb, which is absolutely inaccurate from a scientific point of view, since the notion of the earth as a feminine bosom would be more correct.

Sometimes the image of the pillow is associated with that of the decay of society as the limits of obsolete relations of production, which is inaccurate from a Marxist point of view, since the mechanism of the interaction of the relations of production and the decay of society is fundamentally different.

Because of the difficulties in achieving an accurate ratio between firmness and elasticity this object is virtually impossible to reproduce. For the reasons indicated above, its actual existence is considered unlikely.

Column

Comrades! The column is one of the most prevalent objects in man's social, labor, and everyday activities.

It consists of a purely cylindrical shape mounted vertically in relation to the surface of the earth. In size it ranges from 20 mm to infinity in length.

It is depicted with one finger extended, free end up.

In daily life it is used for power lines, in fences and gates, in the middle of a given space, and so on.

The historical origins of the column are associated with the emergence of communal-clan-based systems, which is inaccurate, since much earlier columns of natural origin have been found.

The image of the column is often used as a spiritual and mystical symbol of male sexual energy of the phallic type, which is absolutely inaccurate from a scientific point of view, since the notion of the androgynous workings of sexual energy would be more correct.

Sometimes the image of the column is associated with that of the role of the individual in history, which is inaccurate from a Marxist point of view, since the mechanism of the role of the individual in history is fundamentally different.

Because of the difficulties in achieving a purely cylindrical shape and absolute perpendicularity in installation, this object is virtually impossible to reproduce. For the reasons indicated above, its actual existence is considered unlikely.

Scythe

Comrades! The scythe is one of the most prevalent objects in man's social, labor, and everyday activities.

It consists of an iron bar fitted onto a wooden handle, one side of which takes the form of absolute circularity. In size it ranges from 20 mm to infinity in length.

It is depicted with an open palm, stretched out at an angle to the axis of the forearm.

In daily life it is used for mowing, cutting, sharpening, fights, popular uprisings, and so on.

The historical origins of the scythe are associated with man's transition to animal husbandry, which is inaccurate, since much earlier scythes of natural origin have been found.

The image of the scythe is often used as a spiritual and mystic symbol of an attribute of death, which is absolutely inaccurate from a scientific point of view, since the notion of death as a river with a ferryman would be more correct.

Sometimes the image of the scythe is associated with that of the dictatorship of the proletariat in the period of transition from capitalism to socialism, which is inaccurate from a Marxist point of view, since the mechanism of action of the dictatorship of the proletariat is fundamentally different.

Because of the complexity of achieving absolute circularity on one of its sides, this object is virtually impossible to reproduce. For the reasons indicated above, its actual existence is considered unlikely.

Wheel

Comrades! The wheel is one of the most prevalent objects in man's social, labor, and everyday activities.

It consists of a piece of wood, iron, or other material in the form of a perfect circumference. In size it ranges from 20 mm to infinity in length.

It is depicted by clamping the free ends of pointer finger and thumb together.

In daily life it is used in carts, cars, locomotives, ships, airplanes, instruments of torture, and so on.

The historical origins of the wheel are associated with the beginning of man's social and labor activities, which is inaccurate, since much earlier wheels of natural origin have been found.

The image of the wheel is often used as a spiritual and mystic symbol of the functioning of life on earth, which is absolutely inaccurate from a scientific point of view, since the notion of life as a light that shines even in the darkness would be more correct.

Sometimes the image of the wheel is associated with that of the constant process of commodity—money—commodity—money—commodity—money, which is inaccurate from a Marxist point of view, since the mechanism of commodity—money—commodity is fundamentally different.

Because of the complexity of achieving absolute circumference, this object is virtually impossible to reproduce. For the reasons indicated above, its actual existence is considered unlikely.

Ape

Comrades! The ape is one of the most prevalent objects in man's social, labor, and everyday activities.

It consists of the absolutely final stage in the evolution of the miscellaneous animal world into the human. In size it ranges from 20 mm to infinity in length.

It is depicted by gripping the hand into a fist with the middle finger slightly pulled out forward relative to the other fingers.

In daily life it is used as an exhibit at the zoo, for scientific research, in name-calling, and so on.

The historical origins of the ape are associated with the evolution of the preceding species into it, which is inaccurate, since much earlier apes of natural origin have been found.

The image of the ape is often used as a spiritual and mystical symbol of the randomness and deceptions of life, its grimaces, which is absolutely inaccurate from a scientific point of view, since the notion of the ephemeral nature of life as *maya*, the real world as mirage, would be more correct.

Sometimes the image of the ape is associated with that of the transition of every social class that was once progressive into a reactionary formation, which is inaccurate from a Marxist point of view, since the mechanism of the regression of social classes is fundamentally different.

Because of the complexity of determining the absolutely final stage of evolution, this object is virtually impossible to reproduce. For the reasons indicated above, its actual existence is considered unlikely.

Woman

Comrades! The woman is one of the most prevalent objects in man's social, labor, and everyday activities.

It consists of the sum of ideal feminine qualities. In size it ranges from 20 mm to infinity in length.

It is depicted by placing two fingers on a surface.

In daily life it is used for love, childbearing, housekeeping, dancing, and so on.

The historical origins of women are associated with the period of man's origin, which is inaccurate, since much earlier women of natural origin have been found.

The image of woman is often used as a spiritual and mystical symbol of life, which is absolutely inaccurate from a scientific point of view, since the notion of life as an impersonal, all-consuming energy would be more correct.

Sometimes the image of woman is associated with that of the amorphousness of the popular masses, which is inaccurate from a Marxist point of view, since the mechanism of the amorphousness of the popular masses is fundamentally different.

Because of the complexity of achieving absolute femininity, this object is virtually impossible to reproduce. For the reasons indicated above, its actual existence is considered unlikely.

Hammer and Sickle

Comrades! The hammer and sickle is one of the most prevalent objects in man's social, labor, and everyday activities.

It consists of an absolutely inseverable combination of hammer and sickle. In size it ranges from 20 mm to infinity in length.

It is depicted by two hands, one of which is compressed into a fist, the other with open palm.

In daily life it is used as a hammer and sickle.

The historical origins of the hammer and sickle are associated with the moment of awareness of the unity of working class and peasant class, which is inaccurate, since much earlier hammers and sickles of natural origin have been found.

The image of the hammer and sickle is often used as a spiritual and mystical symbol of eternal change, which is absolutely inaccurate from a scientific point of view, since the notion of eternal change in the form of a god dying and coming to life would be more correct.

Sometimes the image of the hammer and sickle is associated with that of the mechanical unification of the interests of workers and peasants, which is inaccurate from a Marxist point of view, since the mechanism of the unification of the interests of workers and peasants is fundamentally different.

Because of the complexity of achieving absolute inseverability, this object is virtually impossible to reproduce. For the reasons indicated above, its actual existence is considered unlikely.

OBITUARIES

(1980)

Advisory Note

There is no Advisory Note nor will there be.

It is with deep regret that the Central Committee of the CPSU, the Supreme Soviet of the USSR, and the Soviet government report that on February 10 (January 29 O.S.) of the year 1837, at the age of 38, as a result of a tragic duel, the life of the great Russian poet Alexander Sergeyevich Pushkin was cut short.

Comrade A.S. Pushkin was always distinguished by his upstanding principles, his sense of responsibility, and his conscientious attitude toward himself and those around him. In all the posts to which he was sent, he displayed selfless dedication to his duties, military bravery and heroism, and the noble qualities of patriot, citizen, and poet.

He will remain always in the hearts of his friends and relatives, who knew him as a playboy, joker, womanizer, and mischief-maker.

The name Pushkin will live forever in the memory of the people as the leading light of Russian poetry.

§

It is with deep regret that the Central Committee of the CPSU, the Supreme Soviet of the USSR, and the Soviet government report that on July 15, 1841, the marvelous Russian poet Mikhail Yuryevich Lermontov died, as the result of a duel.

Comrade M. Y. Lermontov was always distinguished by his upstanding principles, his sense of responsibility, and his conscientious attitude toward himself and those around him. In all the posts to which he was sent, he displayed selfless dedication to his duties, military bravery and heroism, and the noble qualities of patriot, citizen, and poet.

He will remain always in the hearts of his friends and relatives, who knew him as a person of difficult and hot-tempered character, a duelist, and visionary.

The name Lermontov will live forever in the memory of the people as the dark genius of the era.

§

It is with deep regret that the Central Committee of the CPSU, the Supreme Soviet of the USSR, and the Soviet government report that in the year 1881 the famous writer Fyodor Mikhailovich Dostoevsky departed from this life.

Comrade F.M. Dostoevsky was always distinguished by his upstanding principles, his sense of responsibility, and his conscientious attitude toward himself and those around him. In all the posts to which he was sent, he displayed selfless dedication to his duties, military bravery and heroism, and the noble qualities of patriot, citizen and poet.

He will always remain in the hearts of his friends and relatives, who knew him as a peevish and suspicious person burdened with serious illnesses and the memory of his years spent in prison.

The name Dostoevsky will live forever in the memory of the people as a seeker of God and a fideist.

§

It is with deep regret that the Central Committee of the CPSU, the Supreme Soviet of the USSR, and the Soviet government report that Count Lev Nikolayevich Tolstoy is no more.

Comrade L.N. Tolstoy was always distinguished by his upstanding principles, his sense of responsibility, and his conscientious attitude toward himself and those around him. In all the posts to which he was sent, he displayed selfless dedication to his duties, military bravery and heroism, and the noble qualities of patriot, citizen and poet.

He will remain always in the hearts of his friends and relatives, who knew him as a big aristocrat, fascinated by the ideas of Buddhism, Tolstoyanism, and living the simple life.

The name Tolstoy will live forever in the memory of the people as a mirror of the Russian revolution.

§

It is with deep regret that the Central Committee of the CPSU, the Supreme Soviet of the USSR, and the Soviet government report that in the year 1980, in the city of Moscow, in the fortieth year of his life, Dmitri Aleksandrovich Prigov continues to live.

APOTHEOSIS
OF THE OFFISSA

(1975–1980)

First Advisory Dialogue

First Offissa: So, what's this oppo-the-osis?

Second Offissa: How to explain? It's kind of like getting an honor.

First Offissa: An honor? Like getting epaulettes?

Second Offissa: Well, no. Not quite epaulettes.

First Offissa: Well, what then? Maybe a medal?

Second Offissa: No, not quite like a medal.

First Offissa: Not really?

Second Offissa: Not really.

First Offissa: So what is it then?

Second Offissa: Well, oppo-the-osis—it's kind of like a certificate of Appreciation.

First Offissa: Aha. Got it.

Second Advisory Dialogue

Offissa: Comrade Major, what's oppo-the-osis?

Major: It's not *oppa-the-osis*, but apotheosis.

Offissa: But what is it?

Major: Ah, how could I explain it to make it easier to under-
                    stand? It is the honest and conscientious performance of
                    your duties, it is serving in such a way that you become
                    an example for others.

Offissa: How long do we have to wait for it?

Major: It depends. If you are especially diligent you might
                    achieve it in five years.

Offissa: And then what?

Major: Then it will last and last and make people happy.

Third Advisory Dialogue

Offissa:	Citizen Author, what's this apotheosis?
Author:	Ah, how could I explain it to make it easier to understand? It is the highest point in this instance of life.
Offissa:	What, it's like the highest rank?
Author:	But for every highest rank, a higher one can be found.
Offissa:	So, it's the very highest rank?
Author:	But the very highest rank can always be trumped by an act of the people's heroism and glory.
Offissa:	So what is it then?
Author:	It is triumph in the face of the limits of impossibility.
Offissa:	How's that? How can you guess what will be impossible further down the line? That can only happen after death.
Author:	Yes, apotheosis is the triumph of life in the rays of ascending death!

§

When here he stands the Offissa on duty
As far as Vnukovo vast expanses open to him
The Offissa looks to the East and to the West
And behind them opens out the void
And the center, where the Offissa stands
The view of him from everywhere is open
From everywhere the Offissa can be seen
From the East the Offissa can be seen
And from the South the Offissa can be seen
And the Offissa is visible from the sea
And the Offissa is visible from the sky
And from underground
                    yeah, but it's not like he's hiding

§

He lives! Among us as before
A knight, whose tale was shared
By Liliencron and after, by Rilke
But after them I alone did dare

See how he strides to his stern post
The Offissa walking his beat
And I sing of him in ecstasy
And my lyre I will not cede

§

So, the Sailor met the Offissa once
And the Offissa told him boldly:
You must be a model for the youth
As I am an ideal model for those older

Take the perspective of the upper limit
To help in comprehending giddy passions
And overcoming momentary fashions
I shall, replied the Sailor, and he did

§

Sitting in the House of Writers bar
The Offissa is drinking beer
Drinking in his customary way
He doesn't even see the writers

But they're all looking right at him
Around him's bright and empty space
And all their different kinds of art
To him mean absolutely nothing

He is truly Life embodied
Appearing in the form of Duty
Life is short though Art has beauty
And in a tussle, Life always wins

§

So they say the Offissa killed somebody
But no, the Offissa didn't kill anybody
The Offissa is constant twixt heaven and earth
It's possible in his private life he killed

There are no accidents in this world:
The Killer's sent to do some killing
The Offissa—to personify the law
But if he kills while in his uniform
It's not the laws of State he's undermining
He flouts the secret laws of all creation
Which earns him metaphysical retribution

§

There is metaphysics in an interrogation
Like take our Offissa, for instance
And a criminal, for example
A green table divides them
But what, pray tell, unites them?
They are united by the Law
Wielding victory above them
Their talk's not carried across the table
It's carried out just through the Law
And in that instant, like in an icon
They are not here—they're in the Law

§

While he was standing there on duty
A field of poppies shot right up
But that field of poppies is there
Because he stood at hand on duty

For when he, the Offissa, would wake
In the morning on days off
He'd come out to the field and touch
The flowers gently with his wing

§

In the middle of the street
Stands the Offissa
He doesn't weep, he does not frown
A model for us all

But who will take responsibility
To make sure he doesn't suddenly
Here at this very crucial moment
Enter the first circle of Hell

§

When the time of misery comes
Elements rising from the depths
And the beasts take out their secret fangs
Who will shield us with his breast?

Well who on earth but the Offissa
Forgetting all his personal comforts
Will rise against the rabble-rousers
Pure and in accordance with the law

§

He prefers life to death
And thus is always on his guard
Whenever he sees death, and even
When she's still under the table

Oh, how well he understands her
How his shoulder senses her approach
Any second now... and yet
He does not try to move his shoulder

§

In the Capital served the Offissa
While she was walking down the street
He was standing tall and proud on duty
She was walking late at night

And at that very moment three
Thugs together ran to her
And they began to menace her
This trio thought, Hey, let's undress her

But the Offissa he saw it all
He came right up and said to them:
You here are breaking our fine law
Immediately you must desist!

She meanwhile gazed and marveled
At his uniform and face
That gaze translated into space
And saw the bright dawn ahead

§

O country! who will understand you and me
Assessed in terms of ever-flowing life
There's the office-worker running through life
The intellectual running from life
The worker drinking vodka for life
The soldier shooting on behalf of life
The Offissa stands in the midst of life
And says, where is the turn
And that turn just goes and stands
There at our very own gate
But the turn exits into eternity
The people hurry—to exit into eternity
The poet stands there, barging into eternity

The scientist thinks about eternity
The leaders try to postpone eternity
The Offissa reins in eternity
And marks it gently in reverse
And again life just goes and stands
There at our very own gate

§

But here he stands the Offissa
Alone amid deserted fields
His station is far from here
Yet in full uniform he stands

He takes his cap off from his head
And looks aloft, and God on high
Descends and kisses his forehead
And says silently to him
Go, child, and be obedient

§

On a boat out on the Oka
The Offissa floats and looks around
To see that no one drowns in the river
Through his own carelessness

And thus 'mid those unfaithful waters
That led so many into temptation
Like some island there he floats
Where we, if stranded, may rest
Our feet

§

A Fireman has laid a fire
The Sailor runs into space
We only have the Offissa
To be our shield and sword

Sailor, he says
Serve the people, brother
And he pours water
Over the red eyes of the Fireman

§

A-walking one day holding hands with his wife
The Offissa's somehow embarrrassed by this
For he, after all, is statehood's representative
And the family too is a unit of that State

And yet it's too close to the grime of the earth
To the flesh and other compromised elements
But he is statehood in all of its purity
Almost so much that it destroys itself

§

The Offissa strides stern and tall
While on his walkie-talkie he
Exchanges communications
Who knows with whom—most likely
With God

And from the heavenly walkie-talkie
Comes a voice truly unearthly:
Oh you, beautiful Offissa!

Be upstanding and forever young
Like a flowering cypress

§

Here stands the Offissa in place
Surveying all around him, committing
All around him to memory, and here his bride
Emergency Aid—flies by all in white
Raising a spray of springtime sheaves
Linking hands they walk together
The heavens melt above them
The ground disappears beneath their feet

§

Somewhere there's a crow out screeching
A baby's sleeping at the dacha
And no one else, the baby sleeps
Alone—where would he go anyway

But if some stranger were to come
And suddenly disturb his sleep
The Offissa will descend from on high
And keep the sleepy infant safe

§

This song was written just to say
That life is beautiful and complicated

Among the half-abandoned skies
Flits a little chickadee

While in an unmowed Moscow ditch,
A knife in his breast, the Offissa
Lies

§

As a child I came to love the Police
And to love them was all that I could do
I grasped their secret essence—
To coincide with human individuals
But for a human to coincide with them
Is tantamount to going mad
Because we are all concrete individuals
When compared to the idea of the Police

§

There where Catullus sits with his sparrow
And Derzhavin with his bullfinch
Mandelstam and his trusty goldfinch…
But who's with me? My dear Offissa's here
We came, looking all around

I am a light shadow, while he's a shadow's shade
So what? But what's wrong with that?
Here all is one, or really, two
Here we're really all just birds

Yes, me, and him, and the Offissa too

§

And now we'll turn to ancient Rome
When Cicero, the ancient Roman,
Opposed Catiline, Enemy of the People

To the people, tradition and the law
Contrasted them to make more clear
The manifest contours of true statehood
And in our time, the Offissa
Stands proud and tall, Rome's equal
Or even greater—an example manifest
That rises above otherwise invisible
Statehood

§

Up there above is Heavenly Power
While here below we have the Offissa
Like, for example, this time, the following
Conversation proceeds between them
"Where are you rushing to, Heavenly Power?"
"Why are you standing there, Offissa?"
"What do you see, Heavenly Power?"
"What have you been plotting, Offissa?"
"Rush on by, Heavenly Power!"
"And you, keep standing there, Offissa!"
"Keep watch, Heavenly Power!"
But it does not answer him.

§

I just lived and died quite simply
Just died—there in the churchyard
For an agonizing, unbearably long time,
Gazing at my now-deceased face,
Stood death in the form of the female Offissa
Full of love and the fulfillment of duty

COMPLETE AND FINAL VICTORY

(1982)

Advisory Note

What is Victory? Well, that's clear enough—victory over the Nazis, victory over Japan, victory over China, and so on. But Complete and Final Victory—that is something mysterious, otherworldly—something from the realm of final truths and aspirations. It is something that is impossible but necessary. It is not the sum of all small victories. It is higher than them. It is already here. It is always here. All of our lives, all our insignificant events—are but reflections of its light.

§

Here stand commanders of production
And here the fighters of the five-year plan
And the soldiers of animal husbandry
And those who are simple, brave at life

Having shouldered all woes
They live at the hidden boundary line
Of that very one, almost already
Complete and final Victory

§

Oh, my people, you are happy
For happy is just what you are
Because you went and hung a slogan
A slogan of great local beauty
What does it mean? What does it say?
Happiness lies in its being hung

§

I so love the people's heroes
Because they are all of the people
And as for the ones against the people
I love them too, and no less
I love them, shall we say, historically
Because everything against the people
Becomes, with time, of the people
And, even now, as we speak, is of the people
And that right there is what I love

§

The more we love the Motherland
The less she's fond of us
So said I on one of these days
And never since has my mind changed

§

On she flows, the beautiful Oka
Amid the beautiful Kaluga
The beautiful people have been sunning
Their hands and feet here since the morning

In daytime off to work they go
To their beautiful black work-station
And in the evening come back again
To the beautiful Oka to live

And this, by the way, may truly be
That beauty, which in a year
Or maybe two, but in the end
Will save with beauty all the world

§

If you would today peer with focused gaze
You'd see that our Pushkin, the one who's a poet
Is really much more like a god of fertility
A watcher of flocks and a father of the people

In every village, in corners benighted
I would erect countless busts of his head
But as for his poems—I'd destroy every one of them
For they diminish the image of the man

§

A hero who's outstanding
Goes forward without fear
But our ordinary hero
He's almost fearless too
But first he takes a moment:
Maybe there's a way around it?
And if there isn't—he goes off
And leaves it all to the people

§

Along the waves, the radio waves
Having lost her external appearance
The livestock specialist Glafira
Is speaking to her country

How excellent her life is
At work—full steam ahead
For her all's clear and easy
She's speaking to her country

And from afar the country hears
From beyond the river, out of sight
But for its noisy breathing
It's silent like some great beast

§

Let's say, here with us in Russia
Revolutionaries are all simple

But then, over there in Cuba
It's like revolutionaries squared

But then Africa or Asia
They just don't fit into any measures at all

§

It doesn't matter that the milk yield as recorded
Does not match up to the real yield
Everything recorded is recorded in heaven
And if it does not come to pass in two or three days
In some years it will certainly come true
And in the highest sense it already has come true
And in a lower sense, all will be forgotten
And is already now almost forgotten

§

Here is Stalin with his Vasily
Both gleaming with medals
And dazzling omnipotence
Evidently, such is their fate

And right they are who say Vasily
Was born with golden epaulets
Of omnipresent omnipotence
Embedded in another's breast

§

The Poles have set their sights again on Moscow
It's understandable, for she's a world capital!
First their Solidarity, then the Junta
And next—they'll come straight for Moscow
Just like in 1941! But there'll be no wrangling
For ancestral Russian soil with them now
No, dear Comrade Jaruzelski
You will not see Moscow conquered!

§

The crowd flies along, sweeping away all obstacles
Dissatisfied for the time being
The Offissa from up on high
Recites, not denying their truth
Nor letting drop his faithful bayonet
He recites:
Oh the mad fury of the wild and bitter truth!
Oh the cold blood of the answering bayonet!

§

I never loved you
And yet I did not kill
And I never respected you
And yet I imprisoned no one
So you all can just go on living here

And give thanks to me
That I didn't love
But didn't kill
Didn't respect
But never sent to prison
And give thanks to me
I didn't kill, after all
And though I didn't love
I didn't sentence anyone
Though no respecting either
So give thanks to me
That you're living now

§

I must say I got used to the climate
In my forty-second year, and I'll say
I now find even some delight
In this cold and in the lighter frosts

But we must admit that the legal order
Given all the signs, would better suit
The tundra or somewhere else up there
While for our latitudes, given all the signs,
It offers really no charm at all

§

Spring is coming—and her victory
Is unquestionable and clear
Like, just look out, right after lunch
And there is spring right outside
And then there's summer right outside
And autumn, and winter too
And that there is complete and
Final victory over everything!

HOUSEKEEPING

(1975–1986)

§

I've spent all my life washing dishes
And composing poems most sublime
And this has lent me all of my life's wisdom
And made my temperament firm and mild

I watch the water flow and comprehend it
Below my window—the people and the powers
Whatever I don't like I simply overrule it
And what I like is all surrounding me

BANAL RUMINATION ON THE TOPIC:
Man does not live by bread alone

If, let's say, we have some groceries
Then we don't have something else
While if, say, we have something else
In that case we have no groceries

If however we have nothing
No groceries or anything else
Nevertheless we still have something
After all, we're here living, reasoning

BANAL RUMINATION ON ECOLOGICAL ISSUES

I have this passion—on the sly
To nibble at (who knows why?)
The bits of two-week-old sausage
Like some kind of vulture pet

But this is, let's say, a kind of gift
In a sense general and more indistinct
I am, like, a kind of a vulture of life
Like, in life I am a kind of a medic

BANAL RUMINATION ON THE TOPIC OF FREEDOM

Just when you've finished up the dishes
Look—a whole new pile awaits
What kind of freedom is this
Just let me make it to old age
True, you could just not wash them
But then various people come by
And say: the dishes are dirty
What kind of space for freedom here

§

Something recently went missing
In our dear semi-processed foods
Or perhaps the time has come
For their decline and disappearance
But maybe there will rise in turn
A wholly different phenomenon
Maybe something otherworldly
Like a quarter-processed food

§

A kilogram of fish salad
I acquired at the deli
Nothing wrong with that
So I acquired it, so what?
I ate a little bit myself
Then my uterine son
I also fed with the stuff
And we sat down at the window
By its transparent glass
Just like two male cats
So life could flow on down below

§

Here's some lovely gummy yogurt
Full of flavor and so filling
Full of the lack of scent
Full of pinkish color too

One might think angels partake of it
On Sundays and church holidays
And then with lucid smiles they poop
Down snow and fog upon the earth

§

Some people don't wash the dishes
And hens' bellies they don't cut open
And still they can sometimes be happy
But for what, why can they, well

Because in that world beyond this one
We will sit at a table so fair
Like little children so pure
But they with their mouths gaping open
Will dash catching our spit from the air

§

I'll drink some Brazilian coffee
And eat a whole Dutch chicken
I'll wash with Polish shampoo
And become the Internationale

And I'll step out onto the Prague streets
And fly into the Pacific Ocean
And all people will become brothers
And O Lord my God forgive me

§

Here I'm standing quietly in line
And thinking partly to myself:
Now Pushkin standing in this line
And Lermontov standing in this line
And Blok, too, standing in this line
What would they write about? About happiness

§

I scored some chuck strips at the deli counter
And headed for home, coddling my bounty

When from behind the case, not hiding in the least,
Heaving an enormous chunk of illegal meat

Out came a filthy decrepit old bitch
That chunk, it was huge—doubt she could lift it

Well, it'd be one thing if she worked at the store
OK then, she's got rights to take a bit more

But no, she was just random, and plus she was ugly
While me, I'm a poet, the pride of Russia, that's me

Half the day wasted standing with strangers
But happiness lives with the likes of these bitches

§

Those bastards kicked me, dammit
Out of line tout suite
I was waiting to get grapes
Thinking I'd have a li'l treat

Nasty women fell upon me
Said I hadn't been in line
Well, I hadn't for the whole time
But I'd sure spent some time
Nearby

§

The beast drags home to his spouse
A steaming-hot blood-covered slab
Just like that I with a bunch of carrots

Drag myself home from the supermarket
A little onion, maybe a turnip
A bag or two of spuds
A little bottle of the strong stuff
To make your head go spinning

§

If the mind-boggling Ovid
The beast of ancient Roman poetry
Came to visit me and saw
Me eating chicken giblets
Or some delightful sweet cake
He would exclaim, out of his long-past life
Was it for this that in the depths of Moldova
I perished and suffered—For this, for this
My sweet

§

I went out for a cake one morning
So I could have guests that evening
But life is such an intricate affair—
Not only such special penchants
As cake, but even simple sweets
And sugar—none were to be had
And then the guests did not come
You might think it was all by chance
But no—those days are now upon us
Which have been gaining for so long
Clearly, fate's breath is felt here in all

§

I'll fry a little cutlet
Cook up a little broth
And put it down to rest a bit
While I open up the window
Out to the courtyard and jump right in the sky
And fly and fly
And fly, and then come back
And eat some if I want to

§

You and me, we'll fry some mushrooms
And eat them with sour cream
And then we'll lie down me and you
And sleep as soundly as can be

And tomorrow we'll get up in the morning
And run off to the forest skipping
And whatever we find there—we'll eat it up
And with a clear conscience head off
Back to Moscow

§

I'll roast a chicken
I really can't complain
And it's not like I'm complaining
What am I—better than everyone else?
And I'm ashamed, made weak
Just imagine—this one
Chicken was my undoing
Done in by my country

§

I'll wash all of the dishes
On a winter evening
Even better at night
When all the house is sleeping

I wash and I remember:
I once ate with that guy
Used to drink with that one
That one once sat with me

And now where are they? Gone
They've all died all to the last
We sat here of an evening
A single evening once

§

The broom is broken, won't do its job
Nothing for me to sweep the floors
But back then, holy shit,
How I once used to sweep
Then, the way I used to sweep,
Brightness would reign over all, but now
Everything's broken, won't do its job
I don't want to live

§

When I would secretly take the garbage
In the evening, so the neighbors would not see
Not far off, by the nearby kindergarten
Since, despicable man, I lacked the strength
To rise at dawn and heed the merciless call
Of the sainted garbage truck—

I was a criminal—O Lord, judge me
Either I die, or at your faintest call
I'll rise

§

I wrestle with domestic entropy
As a source of energy divine
These forces, inglorious and blind,
I overcome in quiet unsung struggle

I'll wash the dishes three times a day
Wash and scrub the floor all over
I'll build the meaning and structure of the world
On this place that seems like it is empty

§

For the last time, friends, I'm living it up
Taking a shower with hot water
But tomorrow—maybe I'll be behind bars
Or in a strange and unknown land
Or maybe it'll all be much simpler
They'll just turn off my hot water
I'll be filthy and indecent
And women won't like me

§

I struggled with this screw all day
And could not get the best of it
There was some thing that that screw knew
And no one else could know it
And I cried out: O Iron God

Go on, live on dissimulating
But this thread does not belong to you
Give it up at least!
But the screw didn't fall for it

§

Hey, listen! Can you hear—it's raining!
No, no, that's the east side crying
All
As if a drain pipe is sobbing
Booming
Or a heavenly kerosene stove singing in the kitchen
As if someone gentle had tied up some knots
And flew off most amiably
To the Kazan Station

§

Water flows from the tap
Clean, transparent, thick
And a hundred other qualities
And what follows from this?
What follows: we must live on
And sew our sundresses from calico
And we really don't want… Go on?
To be imprisoned for our views
But we must

§

Here weeps the piteous washing machine
With all of its feminine clandestine essence
While I as an essence am, like, supermundane

Stand looming above her to bring about triumph
Given that I am unable to do it
And she, though she weeps, does bring it about
And her great humility allows
Me to pass most righteous judgment on myself

§

There's something rotting in that garbage pail
And what's rotting? My very own leftovers
And all for that I might be human
Oh my dears! Oh, sweeties!

Guilty I stand before you!
I'd come and live beside you
But cannot absent my station
I have been put here as a human
For a while

§

Look, he's all set up for laundry
This one poor gentleman
A master of his own fate
But really only fate's plaything

Having mustered all his will, now
He forces himself to do the laundry
Leaving all affairs to languish
And tomorrow, who knows, he might die

§

I've gone and patched my wife's old boot
And without rage of any speeches there
While Pushkin suffered from debt

And Nekrasov withered over a potato
While Reagan hurried on
To put new Pershing missiles in the west
And I patched up my wife's boots
So get started—now we're ready
Me and the wife

§

When, I recall, in his youth I would feed
My son with a plastic spoon
And he would fuss and wouldn't eat
As if he sat in undisguised proximity
To some kind of diabolical horror
I would think: this is certainly a child
And yet he feels me through and through
Well, yes, I'm doing this with love
For him

§

Oh how long ago it was
That I in my sailor suit
Leapt like an infant among people
And from above the sun shone down

But now I seize passersby
By the sleeve: don't you remember, you bastards
How in my fancy sailor suit
I leapt! I did! It was true!
They don't remember

§

He slices up the candy
And puts it on his bread
Oh, my poor sick baby child
Of the post-war years

Were some capitalist
To set eyes on this
He'd be shaking in his
Britches, like a leaf

Here's this baby of the human kind
Who looks just like a beetle
Watch his little sheep's head tremble
Over this one bit of sweetness

§

It was by the Patriarch Ponds
That my childhood passed
And now where am I to go
Since I have grown so old

What sort of ponds will have me
What murky waters will I see
Oh, can it be that in all of Nature
There is no water left for me

§

Of course, it's a shame to die young
But that's by weak and earthly standards
When you get there, out of old age, all crippled
And he's there, all young, holy shit
For all eternity remaining

You'd give up absolutely any limb
To remain for all of that eternity
Young
But it's too late

§

The locksmith goes out to the wintry yard
Looks up—and it's already spring in the yard
And just so, just as he is right now
So he once was a schoolboy, but now he is a locksmith

And further on, all the more—further on is death
But before that—old age
And before that, and before that
And before that—just a locksmith as he is

§

And what is this mud to us? It's cool!
Big deal—you've muddied your feet some
Or else you'll take up laying paths
You'll build them this way, that way, so,
Then you'll start pouring on the asphalt
But then before you know it—you'll just die
Without walking on it

§

For some reason the air today's all bent
So when you set out in one direction
You end up going in another direction
And you won't make it home
Or, sometimes, you do get home—my God!

And your house has gone all bent
And some other direction is where
It's facing

§

I walk along the Garden Ring
Until I come to Nogino Station
My head full of mischief
Has its fate all set

Here I get onto the metro
All the way to my own stop
I get back home, I go to bed
And there she is already sleeping
Full of mischief

§

Little boy, little boy, literate one,
My teacher's pet, Young Pioneer!
Tell me, tell me, tell me quick
What's to become of me?

He answered me: you'll go right away
My dear uncle mine
You'll slip and fall without delay
Right under that bus there!
Thanks, kid

§

The one who runs will surely stumble
Yes and he who walks and he who flies
Yes, the one lying down, and the one sitting

And he who drinks and loves and eats
They'll stumble over the very first bone
Since boy he's really really running
Really walking, lots of lying
Tons of eating and drinking and loving
And that there will do him in

§

I noticed how hard people sleep in the metro
Somehow stupid and vacuous, though sometimes they look young
Maybe life is just like that, or maybe this depth exceeds our human
    strength
This is after all the grave we're talking about
And even more than that—the next world, though they're alive and
    the lights are on
They're just sleeping hard, even though they look alive

§

What a graceful slender little mom!
What a dreadful little son!
Ah, what is this life we lead!
If I could get just an hour alone

But on the whole life is correct
For otherwise these moms might
Forget their obligations
And their rights
And our foundations
Would begin to deconstruct
And what then? We'd all be fucked

§

Though I was ill, my soul did live.
I gulped down tabs of aspirin.
So what then did my soul live in?
I was weaker than a cooked cherub.

But when I started to get better,
I decided I'd set things right
Oh legs, my legs, your awful weakness
Came very close to failing me.

§

Now it is really so unbelievably cold
So cold that nothing's left, not even bones
Then, sometimes, you do find bones
Turns out they're unfamiliar
Or just a pile of shinbones
Something like a fighting cock's—
Maybe it's better that way

§

I'm a little bit dead tired
Probably because I'm tired
I lived my life most tirelessly
But now for some reason I'm tired
Is this why I finally got tired
Or am I just tired of this

And later those songs drone on
Like, in this country we never get tired

§

On a wingèd Sunday
In the wingèd month of May
Some kind of wingèd somethings
With something wingèd winged
I went out of the entrance
Out of my own dear home
Where I'd spent the whole long winter
And with my family too
I went out and I started weeping
I sat, I squatted down
And I could not find the strength
And I did not want to live
See, I had endured all winter
I was thin, but my soul was pure
Then here there was such happiness
And I no longer wanted to live

§

It has been known since ancient times
That man is stronger still than death
While in our own day, believe you me,
Even stronger than life is he

Death, she teases him and tempts
But he just bares his middle finger
He cannot at all be tempted
He revels in his poverty
For he is stronger still than all

§

So many sweet and alluring
And quite respectable maidens
They dance, they dance
Skirts with a leg peeping out

Harmoniously quivering
And with smiles on their lips
They rush past my open arms
And into someone else's—oh!

§

I used to carry such a force inside
That dying was like running to the store
But now I look and find no more
Just to lift a stone takes it all out of me

Was it just some other time, or maybe
It was some other place that I lived
Sometimes you say a word, and you've convinced them
And then whatever you say, you're convinced
To death

§

I'll load up with awful force
And this woman looks at me
She'll say: Oh, so handsome
Love me, fucker!

I will shudder and whistle loud
And just let all that force go
Who knows where

§

Walk fifteen feet away from me
Especially the girls
I'm gonna start swearing
Let out some air into the wind

Why?—just because
Like a sort of life-act of
Salvation

§

I understood how they give birth, oh God
When, like huge stones, feces
Conceived within, moved through my guts
Tearing everything along the way
I howled, I sobbed, I groaned, I sang
And when it finally came forth
I welled up with transparent tears
Over it, but it was dead

§

His movements they were regular
He worked properly, he ate
And drank as well, yet happiness
He had not in his life

Was Fate just extra cruel to him
Or is there just no joy
Or maybe the East's proximity
Or maybe something else

§

You've erected these walls all around you
Hung roofs down from the top
You're locked in and secluded
And up to something shameful

And you don't see, and you don't hear
That from over there your shame
Is visible, like they took the roof off
And are staring right at you

Lift up your eyes—Good God!
Either the criminal should run away
Or first zip his pants
Or first get rid of the corpse

§

There is such force inside me
That if it didn't all leak out
Into the inhuman stink of my feet
I'd have to be a murderer

And everyone avoids me
But if they only knew
They'd run and kiss my feet
That I didn't cut all their throats

§

On a teeny-tiny drop of pus
The comforts of home are fermented.
We are few—we are two! There are three of us!
Maybe we'll be killed tomorrow
Bye-bye-baby

Who needs you, anyway, that you need
To be killed?
You! You yourself will be the ones who kill us!
Bye-bye-by-by-by-by-bye
So, we will, we'll kill you
So what

§

Our life comes to an end
Right at that pole there
And where does yours end?
Oh, yours never ends!
Oh, yours lasts forever!
Congratulations on your life!
How beautiful is your life!
But just how beautiful—we don't know
Since ours is already over

§

Birds are singing happily
In the sky under heaven
And after them various people
Go on singing songs

So life goes on. But yesterday
I thought: We're over!
The end of the world! That's it! Hooray!
We are sometimes mistaken
However

TERRORISM WITH
A HUMAN FACE

(1981)

Advisory Conversation

Terrorist: What is the Truth?

Offissa: The Truth in its human approximation is truth.

Terrorist: And what is truth?

Offissa: The truth is that in the face of which we feel the duty to accept, confirm, and defend.

Terrorist: And what is duty?

Offissa: Duty in its external and objectified form is the law.

Terrorist: And what is the law?

Offissa: Right here and now the law is Me!

Terrorist: So what then am I?

Offissa: You are what has no criterion, is undefined, and unenlightened all together.

§

Kneeling at the entrance to the tomb
It isn't what you imagine—language
No plaster cast, no soulless mask
In it lies a soul, in it lies freedom
In it lies love, in it lies language
Bastards!

§

Here you are, Pushkin, all bronze and quite stupid
But once you were sly as can be, weren't you
Well, I'm alive here, anyway
And walking down Gorky Street
Thinking away: Jeez!
Climbed up on the granite plinth
To direct our poetry!
But then when a terrible bomb
Drops on the city of Moscow
Every single person will be killed
And there'll be nobody to direct

§

In the West the terrorists kill people
Either for money or lofty ideals

But here if anyone even deigns to do that stuff
It's just out of resentment or good old-fashioned rancor

Not for money, not for martial glory
And that is terrorism with a human face

§

In the middle of the universe
Amidst tiny little Moscow
I suffer so from suffering
And am myself infinitesimally small
And if I suffered
Seeing this or that
Then these objects of suffering
Would take on my dimensions
But suffering is suffering
I encompass all the universe
Exceeding even Moscow

§

Why are you biting and barking, dog
Well, let's say, I'm not yours
I'm not your dearly beloved master
But I am still, after all, alive
I have rights too
While you, dog, are nasty, impure
You are a pure terrorist
A diehard Reagan

§

In reflections abstract, but pure—
It was revealed that a match for the Offissa
Has not yet emerged among our Terrorists
That they might both stand forth in glory before Heaven
That they might come together on the expanses of Russia
Like male and female, like fire and ice
And otherwise chimeras pernicious for life will arise
And you stand there, my Offissa, like Don Quixote

§

What kind of monster is this nature
In comparison with the works of this people
Whose plans are birthed of such powerful reason
That they need be brought to completion
While nature, she is scarcely architectonic
Even, on the contrary, she's benighted and chthonic
Brilliant to look at, altogether like a serpent
That steals people away from the State
And pulls them underground and lives with them there
Now wait, you depraved Mother Nature,
The state will arrive and will tear open your belly
And become father to a people unearthed

§

A woman kicked me in the subway
Well, pushing and shoving, what can you do
But in this case she obviously crossed
The line and the whole thing shifted
Into an unnecessarily personal interaction
Naturally, I kicked her back
But immediately begged her pardon
Simply because I was a superior person

§

What means their prattle
When faced with the idea of organizing
The construction of the World Soul
Among those still fully alive
Among children still of the people
In the face of this plan, all are Jews!
Our breast trembles with a shared passion
And with a shared and well-born terror

§

The Americans have launched into space
Their supernew outer space ship
So there, from God's vantage point, they can
Annihilate us with a laser—holy shit!

Well, a sword is one thing, or point-blank
From underground, from under water, from tanks
But from outer space, where there is only God and stars!
Well, I suppose nothing is sacred anymore!
Holy shit!

§

People start off white at first
But under the sun they very quickly
Turn red, and then entirely black
And the same occurs in social life

Thus the laws of man
And dear nature's laws
Are not in any kind of conflict
But actually in legal agreement

§

Life has long left the old woman
The lady's pale but death not arrived—
She's lived by now so many years,
For no real reason, just to be alive

But the youthful rising class
Fears saying: Get gone, old bag!
Since it too
Must find itself in her place
at the time appointed

§

I gave up booze, I'm trying to quit smoking
Don't drink coffee, really, I barely eat
I'm raising myself for the general good
As an easy-going Soviet type

Who will live here and on what—we dunno
Driving all the mean-spirited ones insane
To whom Spartak's no better than Dynamo
To whom freedom's no better than the jail

§

Here stands a military patrol
With a certain hidden thought

Some of our Lord's other favorites
Might find this thought just wretched

But if the army is the body
Of a many-peopled order
This order is then order's order

That is, a pure idea
Embodied in real life
And we live nearby

§

When the years have passed and the currently wild
People have forgotten many things
Fear of me will tear through all of Great Russia
For what I wrote! But it was the truth, after all!
What I wrote
I wrote God knows what
And such fear
And the truth was there too
And fear will tear through all of Great Russia

§

So now they say that our people
Wanted to shoot the Pope
But that cannot be
They're dead to us already
Clergymen, that is
Though, you know, shooting them
Would not be a crime, that is
In that specific sense

MOSCOW AND THE MUSCOVITES

(1982)

Advisory Note

It must be said that the theme of St. Petersburg (Leningrad) has found a fairly complete and appropriate expression in Russian poetry, in conformity with the poetic norms and historiosophical concepts of its time.

This book is an attempt to lay the methodological foundations for the study, by poetic means, of the theme of Moscow, in accordance with the historio-sophical concepts of our time. Like any initial attempt, it may in all likelihood find itself outdated almost immediately.

Well, anyway, may enlightened Moscow become a general monument in our honor.

§

It was cold, and powerful smokes
Entered the sky in orderly columns
The task was to tell them apart from the real
But also give preference to something
And I said to him then: Orlov,
Here is your task—tell them apart from the real
But also give preference to something
And this will be the mysticism of Moscow

§

How beautiful my ancient Moscow
When she stands modestly reflecting
In the bluish waters of the gulf
And reads the dreams of Ashurbanipal
And a hot wind blows in from the south
Carrying the neighboring desert's sands
Swirling through the streets of Moscow
And further, further, higher and higher—up!
To the snow-covered half-naked peaks
From whence rises the Eagle
With a mighty sweep of its regal wings
And looks down, and sees the the white movement
Down below, and folding its wings

It swoops, to meet the snow leopard
All sixteen of its bones and teeth
Bared fiercely and all at once
And the Muscovites follow the terrible battle
And welcome the winner with "Hurrah!"

§

When the scope of Napoleon
Exceeded European dimensions
It was thought: we move Moscow deeper into Russia
It was projected: here, we set a flashing muzzle
There—artillery, here—Bagration
Behind him, the entire magical Russian people
And that's better! Because it's better
In every sense

§

What Moscow is—that's what makes her Moscow
What strikes the stranger unto death
And strikes him so very terribly
That he's left no other choice:
To stay so struck until death comes
Or come over to join us—the Muscovites

§

Everyone tries to insult her
The French, and the Germans, and Chinese
All seek to grasp her by the throat
But she just says to them: Here I am!
And they seem frozen with surprise
And stumble back, stumble back, go away

And only come to their senses back home, groaning:
To Moscow! To Moscow! Retreat! Oh, Drang nach Osten
They run and run—and freeze up again…
As it must be—clearly, God preserves Moscow

§

Who won't you find in Moscow
The Germans and Poles have been here for an age
Chinese and Mongols, Georgians
Armenians, Assyrians, Judeans
It was later that they all dispersed
And founded their own States all o'er the world
By the Yellow Sea, in the Caucasus, in Judea
In Europe, the New World, wherever the hell
But they remember their holy first homeland
And beg to be admitted into Moscow's ancient hands
Moscow takes them back with great affection
But some she does not accept
Since it is still too soon, the time's not right
And has not come: they haven't understood, haven't earned it
Have not matured

§

When ancient Rome on this very spot
Did establish its great state and laws
Clad in togas, Muscovites went to the Senate
Their heads all crowned with laurel wreaths
Now it's jeans and miniskirts of all stripes
But still they are the envy of the world
And under this strange modern clothing
Still beat the hearts of proud Muscovites

§

When the movement here arose
For an independent Moscow
They summoned all at once the Mongols
The Poles, the Germans, and the French
And wiped out the lot of them to the core
But even now occasionally
In a girlish gait, in certain words
There will flash a crazy spark
Of national Muscovite pride

§

When Moscow was still a she-wolf
And ran around the woods outside of Moscow...
It was later that she settled down
And became a first-class capital
That was when she started to have children
That huge tribe of white-toothed Muscovites
To whom alone it was given to see
How in the heavens, from a barely visible point
A flame in snatches suddenly starts growing
It grows, it grows, it billows and goes dim
And takes everyone up to itself in heaven
Moscow stands—but there are no Muscovites

§

When the Muscovites go out for strolls
And have a look at lively slogans
They afterwards will notice right away
That Heavenly Moscow in the heavens
With its views of Rome, Constantinople,
Of Poland, of Beijing, of all creation

And with a view of underground Moscow
Where ferocious fire struggles as it flickers
As it breaks through living cracks
And Muscovites go skipping, as if
Heading for the sky—so they walk through Moscow

§

Now here's the Moscow of my own epoch
Here's Lenin Prospect, and the Mausoleum
The Kremlin, Vnukovo, the Bolshoi, and the Maly
And the Offissa is at his post
In springtime bloom the gardens and the parks
Acacia, cherry, apple trees, and lilacs
Tulips, roses, hollyhocks, and dahlias
The grass, the fields, the meadows, forests, and mountains
The heavens are above here, and down below is earth
In the distance live the Chinese, Blacks, and 'Mericans
Close at heart is the whole world deprived of civil rights
But all around—Moscow keeps growing and breathing
She'll grow to reach Poland, grow to Warsaw
To Prague, to Paris, and New York
And everywhere, if you look without prejudgments—
Moscow is everywhere—its peoples are all over
And where Moscow's not—there's only emptiness

§

When one leaves Moscow, you might as well have died
Both going past its borders, or leaving it completely
Her greatness stuns the soul
And assumes great courage of the soul
But imposes likewise obligations
And these here could not withstand it and moved on
Both Groys and Kosolapov, and Shelkovsky

The Gerlovins and Sokov and Roginsky
Due to their unsurprising human weakness
And they do not deserve the title "Muscovite"

§

When Moscow strikes up a song
And sings with her fearsome voice
Who will dare to out-sing her
All the more, in this place
Well, I will do it—I do not fear
To find myself self-satisfied
But to end up in another place
Now that is what I really fear:
From there you'll not out-sing a soul

§

But what is Moscow—not a girl, or a bird
That we should fear for her every day
She won't fly off and won't disgrace us
She will not marry and will not flee
And she's not wife, or sister, or mother
But a song: if sung—then it exists
But if not sung—well, it still exists
But in a certain otherworldly sense

§

Here's Moscow, the white swan
A black raven coming toward her
Learned in European wisdom
Yet she is innocent and pure
Below there's a knight—he places

An arrow to his bow but unexpectedly
He misses accidentally
And ends up in Moscow!
And he begins to grieve
Walking the empty streets
And he encounters no one
And there he remains to live

§

When the world was washed with waves of mass arrests
And collectivization and genocide was underway
Various Jews who'd saved themselves
And Russians, and Germans, and Chinese
Ran secretly to the forests outside of Moscow
And founded there the city that is Moscow
Subsequently little was heard of it
And no one ever saw a real live Muscovite
Or maybe people are just shameless liars
And it's such a strange name—Moscow

§

Imagine: an enormous giant's sleeping
Then suddenly, in the North, his foot awakens
Everyone in the North goes running to the South
Or, in the South, his hand awakens
And once again, they run from South to North!
And what if all at once there suddenly awoke
The mind, conscience, say, or honor, and intelligence
What will happen! Where can they run?!

§

Sometimes it happens that images most gloomy
For some reason visit the minds of Muscovites
Sometimes it seems to them it's winter
That snow surrounds them, and bitter frosts
But it's important to find the right word
And once again all will be filled with meaning
And the Muscovites may edify their progeny

§

Here our Moscow's been swapped out
And hidden from the poor Muscovites
And She sits underground and weeps
All covered in cupolas and domes
And transparent Parthenon porticos
And Erechtheion's tall statues
And Akhenaten's towering statues
And in the waters of the Nile, the Ganges, and the Yangtze

§

When your sons, my Moscow,
Go forth so beautifully armed
Wherever they look—the Demon's everywhere
Far from them—the Demon! and near to them—the Demon!
Their neighbor is the Demon! and their father is the Demon!
And the Muscovites go forth and banish the specter
And holy Moscow burns again

§

Where two famous chasms shone forth here
O you, my Moscow, stepped forth and closed them with your breast
Only the very edges went on streaming soot and smoke
And woe to those who move you from your place
Embarrassed by the smell that you give off
And the Muscovites shall rise to the defense
And shall strike them down as they save them

§

'Twould be better just not to live in Moscow at all
But just know that somewhere she exists
Surrounded by high walls
High and distant dreams
And gazes looking at the whole wide world
They fly out and confirm
Their own existence and that asserts
Their own existence and that generates
Their own existence in a willing heart
And that there's what it means to live in Moscow

§

Look, Orlov, since we do not live forever
It would be quite shameful to miscalculate
That you and I live on the edge of the world
While somewhere out there Moscow really is
With bays, lagoons, and mountains
With events of worldwide significance
And Muscovites proud of themselves
But no, Moscow persists where we are standing
Moscow will abide where we tell her to do so
Where we put her that's where Moscow is!
That is in Moscow

§

There's no text and won't be any.

§

No text and won't be.

THE IMAGE OF REAGAN IN SOVIET LITERATURE

(1983)

Advisory Conversation

Reagan: Why hast thou disquieted my ashes?

Offissa: Because we want to offer an evaluation!

Reagan: That is the work of God, not man!

Offissa: And it was God who placed us here!

Reagan: Do not ruin this poor soul!

Offissa: You ruined it yourself!

Reagan: O, save me, teach me!

Offissa: No! You were designed thus from the very beginning! And we are just evaluating.

§

Why does Reagan so torment us
Allows us neither life nor sleep
Die, you rotten, stinking leader
And you damn 'Merican slut

So here he is, in scabs and shit
In pus, in blood, in mange
And anyway, whatever else
Would you expect from him

§

It's hard for us to live with Reagan
He keeps on wanting to defeat us
You madman! Go defeat yourself!
'Cause otherwise it might turn out
You might require our assistance
To help you to defeat yourself

§

So they've elected a new President
Of the United States
And blasted the old President
Of the United States

But what do we care—like, the President
Of like, the be-nighted States
But still it's interesting, this Prez
Of the United States

§

When China attacked the Vietnamese
Our press condemned the former
But me, I wouldn't go condemning them
After all, they're poor people too

They're all just tools in the hands
Of objective historical forces
God punished them by making
Them Revisionists—even if they're against it

§

Our Anatoly Karpov has routed the enemy
Who cunningly reasoned stupidly
Just so, the glorious warrior Karatsupa
Fought the foe with his dog at the border

Just so the vile enemy was routed by Karpov
Heavily, finally, and for all to see
The Japanese fleet at Tsushima
Was sunk just so by the Varyag of legend

At Borodino and at Kulikovo
Just so did the people of Rus rise up again
And the foreign cowards fell in fear
Rose the sun after them
And after them rose a new enemy

§

The swan, the swan, it flies
High above the Soviet land
But the raven also flies
High above the Soviet land

Oh you, swan-like Voroshilov
Oh you, raven-Beria
Oh, my country, oh, the bride
Of eternal certitude!

§

Far off's long-suffering Afghanistan
While close by's my long-suffering people
From one long-suffering place to another
Like a gift an airplane flies

And on the plane are military units
And in the military units sit the people
The people—well, they're always partly lazy
If you don't drive 'em they won't go on their own

§

They don't love us anymore
The way our Stalin loved us
They don't ruin us anymore
The way our Stalin ruined us

Without his ladylike caresses
His manly cruelty
We'll soon be like some sort of 'Merican
Mixing boredom up with bliss
Unable to tell them apart

§

Now that American President
Yearns for a second term
While the simple Soviet dissident
Doesn't even want a first

What draws him to this term
Strangely enough—same as the President:
Everyone in the world is at his own post
And it's not in our power to overcome it

§

So they sat the two of them
On that very branch
One was Lenin-Lenin
And the other was Lenin-Stalin
They conducted quietly
This conversation so
And their wings to the ends of earth
Sent the wind aflowing
This was that far eastern corner
Of the western lands
In the middle of the world
Branches on the edge

§

The Georgians have their Rustaveli
While we have Pushkin facing him
If brought together who will win?
It just must be Rustaveli
But no, it'd be Pushkin, after all
He's backed up by a whole huge nation
But we're all brothers! Come on, let's better
Go and turn our cannons round
Against the common enemy

§

In any ugly awful act
There's always something good
Like take the people's hero Razin
With his abandoned princess
Razin threw her into the Volga
A living daughter of fair Persia
At first glance it's an awful act
And yet it's lovely and poetic

§

Civilians—all of them in the States
And Uniforms—here in the Union
If there they're in service
Here they're in uniform, for example
That's one way to state the case
Take off the uniform and they're all the same
And among us, we put them all together
Like any sort of vocation
Sweet, painful

§

Here Dostoevsky did recognize Pushkin:
Fly, he said, little bird, to the horizon
And later I'll tell you what you should do
To make us two cheerier in the gulag

And Pushkin, he answered: Begone, cursed one!
The poet is free! He knows none of your shame!
What does he care for your nitpicking suffering
Wherever God wants him—He shepherds him well!

§

Our Shostakovich, young Maxim
He fled to Germany
Oh Lord, what is this mania
To flee not to us, but to them
And furthermore, to Germany

And if you think about it right
Then that symphony of his pa's,
The Leningrad one, is really pointed
Against the scoundrel-son
That's what you get

§

Another President chopped down
True, this time out in Bangladesh
There's no salvation for them here,
The Presidents, on our barbaric planet

Everyone supported him, didn't they?
But apparently not everyone. And why?
Oh God! Just a year ago
We dreamed of a President
That we could keep, preserved

§

Over there among the French
There's Mitterrand, Napoleon
But us, meanwhile, we have Kutuzov
It's a pity that he died

But who will have to help us next
When once again we lure them in
But they don't want to be lured—too bad!
So we ourselves will have to go

§

To get a military regime established
You really should turn off the sewer system
And not a single civilized nation
Will stand up to that

When the fecal matter flows out
For the spirit of struggle is by nature proud
It will suffocate in those piles of shit
And utterly die out among the people

§

Who's that there among the branches
Standing half-naked and pale
And singing out so powerfully
Like a winter nightingale

Oh, don't make anything of it!
We have this one guy here
That is, Alexander Pushkin
The Russian androgyne

§

Reagan does not want to feed us
Well, he made a big mistake
For it's only over there they think
That to live we must intake

But we, we do not need his bread
We will live off our ideas
He'll stop and ask: Where are they?
But we're already in his heart!

§

Let's say the Chinese attack
Us with a war—what would happen?
Who would win that sort of thing?
Yeah, the Chinese will probably win
But, maybe, it's our boys who will win
But overall, it's friendship that will win
For we're fraternal peoples after all

§

The case for peace has been most thoroughly lost
And all because God does not want us
To settle at a distance from our enemies
He keeps on settling them right next door
Say, here we are, good friends with Argentina
But what if we were settled next to them
Here, we're plopped down next to China
How can peace and happiness come

§

We go around, do a little voting
In the courts and in the district councils
So how on earth did it turn out
That Reagan got elected President

It seemed like all had been anticipated
Which means that in our system
There must be some little weak spot
Where he came crawling through

§

They live without awareness that
They're reactionary
Well, you can understand them
But forgive them—no way

Or rather, they can be forgiven
But never understood:
For they are reactionaries
Yet live so easily

§

Reagan does not want his pipes
To be ours, so that Soviet gas
Can flow, representing us,
Through the pipes to the West
Well
This little thread will break
But in essence it's undefeated
Like life, like light, like a song to them
It will itself, without these pipes, break through —
Our gas

§

Can it be, that, say, the Latvians
And Lithuanians, various Estonians
Can take deep into their hearts
Russia as their mother dear
Such that they feel great love
Of course—what's stopping them

§

So what? Guys like this get born
Whatever they want, they manage to get it
They'll beat the Canadians and thwack Korchnoi
And we expect nothing less of them

Since they're with the people! And if they beat one
Of ours—right back into the people he'll be enfolded
As if he never was! While over there when they beat someone
He stays lying in the road for a long time

§

The Poles just can't come to their senses
They keep on staging demonstrations
But life is meanwhile passing by
like a quiet madwoman
She keeps on going, restless one
And sometimes stops by at our place,
But now completely mad

§

We are all Mitterrands
Our wounds they torment us
The Socialist torment
We are all Socialists
Here are the Communists
Let's learn from them
But then the Communists
Say to the Socialists:
No one can teach you!
You have no conscience
Class conscience, that is

§

Now our Soviet UN representative
Has once again remained there in America
And he clearly understands from what
He's now to be forever separated
Yet in fact, he understood it earlier
When he quite effectively represented
Us at the UN

§

With villainy, Peter the Great
Did torment his own little son
In the midst of all of Russia
Tormented him with all his might
That son took it, took it, took it
And then in a birch-tree grove
Two hundred terrible years later
In the form of Pavlik Morozov
Finally took his revenge

§

I am not fond of women, though
Now and then their scheming charms me
Like, Furtseva as Minister of State
And Thatcher, leader of a country

The rest, they run, they run, but where?
Emancipated ones, where to?
While we run like Akutagawa
Have you read *Rashomon*? That's where

§

Take Hissène, you know, Habré
And Goukouni Oueddei
Or Gaddafi and Mitterrand,
Reagan and Carter—who is braver?

I'm the bravest of them all
I sit here writing God knows what
I suffer, suffer, and for naught
No reason
Just to be clever

§

Like, let's take Japan
It's forgotten everything

You say Viking, I say Tsushima
So we'll just lay it out real simple:

Bite me
And then all sorts of any bitch
Will be there

§

Washington he left behind
And went off to make war
So that the land of faraway Grenada
Would go to the Americans

And there he watched
The moon rise up on high over Cuba
And through their beard those lips
Did whisper:
Fuck
You!

§

Here it comes, here it comes—the end of the world
Tomorrow we'll get up in our negligée
We'll get up, we'll stand up—and there's no light
There's no truth! there's no money!
And nothing sacred!
Reagan's already in Syria

OPEN LETTER

(to my contemporaries, colleagues, and to all of mine)

(1984)

Advisory Note

There is no advisory note and there will not be one.

Dear comrades! To you, I am talking to you, my friends!

This message is not the fruit of an initial impulse, like the random gust of a sudden breeze, the impulse of a frivolous, fleeting, albeit pretty human existence, excusable through its clear weakness, the impulse of a soul painfully wounded by the terrible frankness of the phenomenal and the impermanence of those beings dearest to our hearts, met for an agonizingly short time among boiling-cold waves rising to terrifying heights unassailable by the human eye and disappearing in the mad gapings of the lower depths, invented by someone's malicious and mercilessly insidious imagination, waves of eternally self-annihilating, self-consuming existence, which was revealed to me with piercing clarity and candor while I lay quiet and attentive, dying, reverently surrounded by grandchildren, great-grandchildren, and great-great-grandchildren, and other related relatives of my line, among whom could be found elders, gray and doddery, as well as infants, pale and frightened, their eyes black and wet from the horror and incomprehensibility of the goings-on, when I looked at them with my gaze, transparent as crystal, already elevated to different heights and spaces, already flown off to some other princely service: and so this message is, on the contrary, the fruit of long and painful reflection and doubts, bred in the most secluded secret lair of a warm-breathing soul and in the cold, glowing crystal-phosphorescent, cosmic, distant, expanding spheres of impassive and incorruptible consciousness, that flee from us and from each other in their desire to reach the elusive boundaries of this world.

My friends! Companions of my doubts and fond, complicit witnesses of minutes of soaring revelations! Compeers! Kinsmen! Fellow tribesmen! We are few. We cannot be many. We should not be many. We are Sudras! We are Brahmins! OM! OM! We are a small tribe, a chosen tribe, called to life from nothingness solely by the close attentions of heaven, destined to fulfill some task generated by our own selves, the only task, not mandatory for anyone in its ruinous detachment from the world of natural habits, affairs and comforts, but inevitable in its voluntary tonsure, acceptance of pure humility of service in the face of those not even looking in our direction, not even turning in profile towards us in half-animal curiosity, not accepting us, not knowing and not wanting to know us, denying the actual grounds for the very possibility of our existence, denouncing us and spewing blasphemy and denunciations upon us, persecuting and punishing us by lopping off our delicate extremities, underdeveloped for communication with the realities of concrete reality, but through the secret hand of that same Providence that arranged and placed us here, waiting for our revelations, sometimes incomprehensible to them in word, sound, and essence, our utterances and verdicts with their instantly-annihilating, sermon-on-the-mountish and historically-revelatory irreversible truth. Oh, their strength is invincible, it is unknowable, for it is not comparable with the power that accepts the people of flesh and of this life. And we knew such a one as this! And we know it now! And something like that happened to me when, wearing a severe Marshal's uniform with laurel embroidery and in full regalia, to the howling and devilish whistling of enemy shells aimed right at me, I threw countless heroic masses at the tall, sharp, and impregnable walls of Berlin, lost in the heavenly expanses, wet from the waves of the nearby raging stormy sea, when tall, thin and steadfast I pressed my parched lips once to the wall and established through the heavy, indeterminate-necessity of mutually revolutionary time, or when I gazed slowly from the icy crest of gleaming Everest through 25x binoculars onto the sights of the tiny visible world—O my brothers, this is all dust, the dust on their feet, knocking off their feet. My friends, that is not what I am here to say!

My dear ones, we know all this, we know all of them, we know how they look, their appearance, their expressions, all the ins and outs. But we do not know ourselves. Yes, yes, yes, yes, yes, Yes! We do not know ourselves! Who, other than us, will look into each others' eyes, who will declare themselves to each other and in the totality of these discoveries, their volume, quality, objectivity and history, will reveal all of us together as a kind of providential organism, the sum of its existential manifestations and achievements, the service of each of us individually. This service is given to us both as a sort of contribution to the common cup of sacrificial offerings, but also as a sort of separate societal workload. Sometimes as a burden, a deadly burden. Sometimes even as death itself. When, I recall, I was sitting on the ice, covered in my own excrement and the excrement of rats, sitting in that deep icy sack that ruined all my youthful flowering and possible subsequent health due to the ill will and demonic malice of the cursed Nikon, that dog, that ragged bitch, that fucking pederast. How I suffered, how was tormented, my God! After all, I was still just a boy, a fragile youth, a foolish child, beardless and naive. But I had strength. God gave me strength. And I had my mind. And my anger. And faith. So, Nikon, fuckin' whoreson, take a bite! What, bitch, you don't like it? Look what you wanted! It'll cost you! Like this! Piece of shit! And remember red-hot Irina the Bear, remember? That's right, before the final rising of man from the dust to heaven you'll be in your coffin, writhing in shit, gulping down feces and urine with your filthy hairy mouth! Do you remember Alepard Sambrevich with his who knows what? No use reminding people so fucked in the head. Or dunking their heads at Polodino and Vlasov? Or Nikishkin's bits of bread? That's right, bitch, you piece of shit! You'll rot for that, you stinking dog, you'll end up headless. You've signed your own order to be drawn and quartered.

My dear ones, I call you, and I forewarn you—neither our enemies, nor our friends will forgive us for this. The enemies will say, "A-ha-aaa!" and our friends will say: "What's wrong with them?" No, no, it's not explanations, not theories or immensely phantasmagoric thoughts, not interpretations of works and other material detritus of our spiritual revelations (they speak for themselves) that history longs for from us, the history of variously-thinking but definitively-oriented people. There are plenty of explanations and interpretations already inside our own works, such that any attempt by interpreters, known to me as of now, adds but little, and is only an attempt to become a congenial cousin—so be that cousin yourself! No, no, and no—hagiography, a new hagiography—this is what I dream of as a true response to the call of history. And its call is irresistible, it even sometimes afflicts me to a fault, I've felt it even from early childhood, when in the heavy, grim war years of winter 1940, pale and shrunken down to the tendons from hunger, my head dangling like a lead weight on a string, dirty, shabby, covered in sores and ulcers, bleeding yellow pus, lymph, and clotty blood blackening right before me, I would collapse to the ground, wheezing and tossing my head back in convulsive jerks, I would be picked up by my father's people, wrapped in furs, down, and cloths, and carried into the house, brought in by the creaking steps of the carved porch into the dark chambers, where my wet nurse sighed and gasped, chasing the girls to bring basins with hot water and milk with honey sparkling yellow at the bottom of the crystal vessel, sent the coachman Arkhip for the Doctor, while at the foot of the bed, smiling from a distance, as in a dream, misty, like a northern or southern mirage, a Fata Morgana, a pale-blue smile lit up the face of my mother with her tall hairdo like a streaming waterfall of golden hair, the long probing beams flashing on the quivering facets of the gems in her invisibly pierced earlobes and around her slender, defenseless, plant-like neck, the long, low-cut dress in which she, swaying slightly in the warm, upward flowing air, raised her thin, pale arm with its slightly translucent blue veins under the surface of her marble-white skin, she opened the lily of the pale-blue surface of the forgotten Tsarskoye Selo pond, opened and waved the hand clutching its batiste handkerchief, making a barely perceptible movement: Farewell!—And sailed off to the distant, heavenly ball, just barely visible or audible from here, but unreachable by any force of the soul, the heart, the tears of memory and wailing. That's how it was.

My friends, we are subtly slipping away from each other along taut strands of living time in directions unknown to us—and it is inevitable, and it sad, and it is wonderful, it has always been so, so it will be, and so it should be. Let us love each other, we will become the diamonds of each others' hearts, but not the hearts of flesh—the hearts of the soul, hearts of the spirit, hearts of creation and of the works of the spirit! Let us write about each other, to become the heroes of each other's works. No, do not write about yourselves, no, don't think of it, do not become proud, we will not make these efforts for our own sake, even in that pure and sublime form proposed by the poet: "Let us give each other compliments?" Not that either. When he, I recall, came to me and said: Here, only you deserve this, take it! I said: No! But not from ingratitude and the callousness of an unperceptive heart—no. Even now I still say: No! I'm talking about something completely different.

I'm talking about how, for example, does anyone know that Kabakov spent his youth in the very heart of the industrial Urals, where as a powerful and raging manual laborer in the "30-year" coal mine he acquired his first impressions of the secrets of life, that Bulatov was born in an ancient Pomor family and until he was 15 years ate only raw meat and bitter roots, that Rubinstein's father was a legendary commander of a glorious cavalry and was the first to introduce writing and the alphabet to the then-wild frontiers of Kalmykia and Tungusia, that during his short and unexpected stint in the Navy, among the raging waters and tornadoes of the Mediterranean Ocean, Orlov saved the life of his immediate superiors, and what if we start talking about Sorokin, or about Nekrasov, or about Chuikov, or about Alekseev, or about Monastyrski, who spent his whole childhood and youth in the wild Altai forests, raised by bears and fed with the milk of mountain eagles, while Gundlach, for example, remembers his ancestors back seventy generations, who wore full-pressure space helmets and spoke a language that no one understood but Gundlach. All of this should not be lost in vain for posterity, but should become a common, universally accessible legacy, lofty models to be emulated and which evoke secret amazement.

My friends, I love you all—Orlov, and Lebedev, and Kabakov, and Bulatov, and Vasiliev, and Nekrasov, and Sergeev, and Gorokhovsky, and Chuikov, and Rubinstein, and Monastyrski, and Sorokin, and Alekseev, and Shablavin, and Kiesewalter, and Ponyatkov, and Makarevich, and Gundlach, and Zvezdochetov, and Mironenko, and Mironenko, and Popov, and Yerofeyev, and Klimantovich, and Velichansky, and Gandlevsky, and Soprovsky, and Sergeenko, and Lyon, and Eisenberg, and Saburov, and Koval, and Backstein, and Epstein, and Rappoport, and Patsyukov, and Akhmetiev, and Abramov, and Safarov, and Shcherbakov, and Evropeytsev, and Novikov, and Dmitriev, and Roshal, and Zakharov, and Albert, and Zhigalov, and Ovchinnikov, and Faibisovich, and Bogatyr, and Bruskin, and Chesnokov, and Schatz, and Rizhenko, and Chachko, and Schenker, and the female gender, and other Muscovites, not mentioned due to the natural weakness of human memory for dates and people, and Leningraders, and the citizens of Odessa, and Kharkov, and Lvov, and Parisians, and New Yorkers, Estonians, Lithuanians, English, Germans, Chinese, Japanese, Hindus, the peoples of Africa, Asia, near, far, middle and other European and Latin American peoples.

I love you, my dears!

TWENTY STORIES ABOUT STALIN

(c. 1975–1985)

I

In childhood, Joseph Vissarionovich Stalin was seriously ill and did not start walking until he had reached 14 years of age. But after six months, through will-power and constant training, he was able to lift very heavy weights. One day he went out and saw a big boy beating up a little kid. Stalin drove off the offender. The boy said, "Truly, you are strong." Stalin looked straight at him, became very serious and replied: "It is not I, but truth that is strong."

II

Things had gotten really bad for the people. One day Lenin came to Joseph Vissarionovich, and said "What is to be done?" Stalin looked straight at him, became very serious and replied: "What is to be done…? Just do it!"

III

One day Joseph Vissarionovich raised up the people and overthrew the Tsar. There was happiness. Grand Duke Constantine came to Stalin and said: "Make peace with us, and the world will be yours." Stalin looked straight at him, smiled wearily, and said: "We do not need the world, Russia will be enough for us."

IV

One day Joseph Vissarionovich entered Berlin in a tank. Explosions all around, shells bursting. A German came running towards him, recognized Stalin and screamed: "Stalin is coming! Oh Lord, have mercy on me! "Stalin looked straight at him, smiled wearily and answered: "The Lord will not have mercy on you, you do not deserve it. But Stalin will have mercy." And he ordered the German released.

V

One day Joseph Vissarionovich was walking around the hospital and saw an emaciated wounded soldier lying in bed and saying to his neighbor: "Stalin is our strength." Stalin looked straight at him, became very serious, and replied: "If Stalin is your strength, here I am. Get up and go." The soldier rose, took his rifle, and walked off.

VI

One day, returning from the campaign, Joseph Vissarionovich dismounted from his horse and wiped his sword on his greatcoat. Anka the Machine-Gun Girl ran up to him and shouted: "We injammered the Whites!" Stalin looked straight at her, became very serious and replied: "Oh, Anka, Anka, how many times have I told you that there is no such word as 'to injammer.' We must respect the great Russian language."

VII

Joseph Vissarionovich was of gigantic stature; he was even somewhat embarrassed by his huge hands. Once he entered a room where Trotsky, Zinoviev and Bukharin were sitting, themselves robust strapping men as well, bending horseshoes. Stalin tore a horseshoe in half and threw it away. Then he looked straight at them, became very serious and replied: "The true measure of one's strength is through work."

VIII

One day Joseph Vissarionovich worked through the night and thought up a plan for defeating the fascist hordes. When he came home they told him that his wife had died. Stalin looked straight at the corpse of his wife, became very serious, and replied: "A man is victorious on the grand scale, but life takes revenge on him through trivialities."

IX

One day Trotsky, Zinoviev, and Bukharin came to Joseph Vissarionovich and said, "It's time for you to go." Stalin opened the window; outside the people were shouting: "Stalin! Stalin!" Stalin looked straight at them, became very serious, and replied: "I will go to them, to the people." And he went out of the Kremlin.

X

Things had gotten really bad for the people. One day representatives of the people came to Joseph Vissarionovich and said: "Come back. We have hung Trotsky, Zinoviev, and Bukharin. They were mistaken." Stalin looked straight at them, became very serious, and replied: "You shouldn't have hung them. How will they find out now that they were mistaken?"

XI

One day Joseph Vissarionovich went to the front line. The Marshals, Generals, and Adjutants ran after him but could not keep up. A soldier ran up to Stalin and said, "You could be hit by a shell!" Stalin looked straight at him, smiled wearily and replied: "I could, but I don't want to."

XII

Joseph Vissarionovich's favorite song was "I will die, I will die." One day Radek sang it in Stalin's presence. Stalin asked him: "Have you carried out my instructions?" "No." Stalin looked straight at him, became very serious, and replied: "The right to sing a song must be earned."

XIII

One day there was a meeting of the Supreme Soviet, both Presidium and Plenum at the same time. The Deputies were sitting there, along with famous people and heroes. And then Joseph Vissarionovich entered through the back door. Voroshilov ran up to him and said: "All kinds of important tasks await us." Stalin looked straight at him, became very serious, and replied: "You're lucky, these tasks await you. I, meanwhile, have been awaiting one important task all my life."

XIV

One day a conversation about Pushkin was underway in the presence of Stalin. Budenny said: "After Stalin, I came to understand Pushkin better." Stalin looked straight at him, smiled wearily and replied: "But Stalin too cannot be understood without Pushkin."

XV

One rainy night Joseph Vissarionovich was out walking and saw an old man without a coat, thoroughly soaked. Stalin took off his cloak and threw it over the old man. The old man asked Stalin: "Hey there, Comrade, who might you be?" Stalin looked straight at him, became very serious and replied: "If I can help everybody like this, I will be a real human being."

XVI

One day Joseph Vissarionovich's son was brought to him and he was told that the boy had stolen a purse from a poor woman. "It's alright" Beria said soothingly, "we have already returned the purse." Stalin looked straight at him, became very serious, and replied: "You've returned the purse, but my son cannot be returned to me," and shot him on the spot with his own hands.

XVII

One day Joseph Vissarionovich was working hard in the Kremlin until late at night. He called his wife and said, "Come on, let's take a walk." They walked, and his wife said: "Why are you torturing yourself? Have a rest. Take care of the children." Stalin looked straight at her, became very serious and replied: "I *am* taking care of the children."

XVIII

One day Joseph Vissarionovich was walking in Red Square. Some kid ran up to him and asked, "Uncle, fix my bike." Stalin looked straight at him, smiled wearily, and repaired the bicycle. The kid said, "Come here tomorrow, I'll introduce you to my mother, she's really nice." Stalin looked straight at him, became very serious, and replied: "I can't, kiddo, it's about time for me to go." And the next day he died.

XIX

One day the Americans, by treacherous means, captured an enormous number of the Russian people. They set the following condition: if you do not turn over Stalin, all will be slaughtered. Zhdanov said to Joseph Vissarionovich, "Do not go, they have prepared a shameful death for you." Stalin looked straight at him, became very serious and replied: "It isn't death that beautifies a man, but man that beautifies death." And the next day they sent him to America, where he was slain, and the people were released.

XX

One day there was a rumor that Joseph Vissarionovich had died. A delegation came to him and, glad to see him alive, said to him: "We would have given our lives, if only that you would live." Stalin looked straight at them, smiled wearily, and said: "And I will give my whole life for you."

SEVEN NEW STORIES ABOUT STALIN

(c. 1985-1990)

1.

One time in Stalin's childhood he and a pal were walking past a butcher shop. Stalin grabbed a piece of meat and they took off running. They were chased down and questioned. Stalin was asked: "Was it you who stole it?" "No," he answered, "it was him." And right then and there they tore his pal to pieces.

2.

Things had gotten really bad for the people. They started rioting. The Tsar summoned Stalin and said: "Get the people to go out on Senate Square." Stalin brought the people out, but the gendarmes were there. They started shooting and all the people were killed. More than a million.

3.

One day Trotsky, Zinoviev, and Bukharin came to Stalin and said, "You're mistaken. Let's have a talk." Stalin grabbed a gun off his desk and shot them on the spot. And ordered that the bodies be buried immediately.

4.

One day Stalin came to see Lenin in Gorky. He saw that there was no one around and cut Lenin down. And he buried the body without being seen. He went back to Moscow and said, "Lenin is dead. He left everything to me."

5.

One day Stalin's wife came to see him and said: "Why did you take all the money away from that poor woman. That's not right." Stalin grabbed a gun off his desk and shot her on the spot. And ordered that the body be buried immediately.

6.

One day Nikita Sergeyevich Khrushchev came to Stalin and said: "You're mistaken. Let's have a talk." Stalin grabbed a gun off his desk, but Khrushchev managed to shoot first and killed Stalin. And ordered that the body be buried immediately.

7.

One day Stalin was walking down the street. The people recognized him and shouted: "Look, there's Stalin!" Stalin took off running, and the people ran after him. They chased him down, tore him to pieces, burnt him, and threw his ashes into the Moscow River.

THE CAPTIVATING STAR
OF RUSSIAN POETRY

(c. 1975-1985)

A poet can do nothing without his people. The poet's popular roots lie in the people, and the poetic roots of the people lie, again, in the people. All this was clear to the great Russian poet Alexander Sergeyevich Pushkin.

At that time there reigned a complicated domestic and foreign policy situation. Napoleon had surrounded Russia, blockaded all its ports and main roads, and was preparing to attack our Motherland. And inside the country, in her very heart, her capital, in ancient Petersburg, with the connivance and direct assistance of the Tsarist court and government officials, the French ambassador de Heeckeren and his nephew were promoting the decadence of Russian society in favor of French influence. All the highest circles already spoke only French, with perfect accents, even to the French ear, and the Empress herself was in correspondence, also in French, with Voltaire, one of the instigators of the French Revolution, which later developed into the dictatorship of Napoleon. A small handful of politically ignorant youth, with the connivance of the authorities, succumbed to propaganda and, at that difficult and dangerous moment, came out onto Senate Square with pro-French, anti-popular slogans calculated to polarize Russian society even as it faced imminent invasion.

Only Pushkin understood the danger looming over Russia. Whenever he could, he denounced Napoleon, that apocalyptic beast, along with the cowardice and corruption of high society, which was trying to avert its gaze from the impending catastrophe on a global scale and quieted its fears with balls and receptions, welcoming Napoleon's protégé and agent de Heeckeren with open arms, he who did his utmost to denigrate everything Russian, particularly the great Russian poet, seeing in him a sole but powerful opponent, thanks to the support of the lower levels of society. The Napoleonic agent incited Chaadaev to write his notorious philosophical letters, in which he slung mud at Pushkin and the entire Russian people, saying that it wouldn't be bad to end up as subjects of the French, calling them a progressive and cultured nation.

And at this point, without declaring war, Napoleon crossed the borders of our state and began to press deep into the territory of our Homeland. But Pushkin decided to lure the usurper into the depths of the Russian snows, rightly expecting that the French, compared to sturdy Russian men, would show little forbearance and be unaccustomed to suffering. Pushkin decided to allow him to get a little closer, and meanwhile toured the vast expanses of his Motherland urging the people to prepare to fight the invaders: dig trenches, collect weapons and Molotov cocktails, burn their crops and never surrender.

De Heeckeren and his nephew then decided to take direct action against the poet. They knew of the great poet's tremendous intolerance toward any kind of poor conduct or crude attitudes towards women. One day all of the upper crust had gathered at a ball. They talked only of the latest news from Paris, about art exhibitions, literary journals, as if all of great Russia could provide nothing acceptable as a topic of conversation or argument. Pushkin entered, tall, blonde, with delicate hands, and, surveying all this cosmopolitan society, he said in a ringing voice: "Gentlemen, Napoleon approaches."

Everyone exchanged uncomfortable glances, as if he had blurted out some nonsense in front of a foreigner. But de Heeckeren's nephew, small, swarthy as a monkey, with a face recalling either a Negro or a Jew, suddenly tripped the great poet and slipped off like a little beast into the crowd of guffawing high-society loafers. Pushkin got up, clenching his fists, but he understood that the French stooge had deliberately provoked him in order to cause a scandal. He wanted a duel so that he could somehow underhandedly kill him. No, this shall not be—thought Pushkin—the people need me, and the honor of the people is above personal honor.

Heeckeren's nephew flitted through the crowd, whispering something in everyone's ear. There he was with Potemkin, and then with the Empress herself. And Pushkin was banned from the home of his friends Küchelbecker and Baratynsky.

Pushkin left this stifling atmosphere and stepped out into the fresh air, and there the simple people had gathered, recognized the poet, were delighted, and said:

"Master, the French will not allow us to live, the villains have taken all our money and land away. They weary us with theft and torture us with blows. The French are a plague on the Russian people. "

And Pushkin answered, "Take heart, brothers. God has sent us this trial. And since he has sent it, he must believe that we can survive the trial. A great future awaits Russia, and we must be worthy of it. "

"Thank you, master," answered the people.

At that moment a messenger made his way through the crowd and said that the British had already landed in Murmansk. The great poet then made the sign of the cross over the crowd, appointed as leader his faithful companion, Vissarion Belinsky the Furious, embraced him, kissed him three times, and sent him against the British. But he still intended to lure Bonaparte in, to allow him to approach closer.

Alexander Sergeyevich returned again to the hall. And there the talk was all about how the Russian people cannot compare to Western culture or history, that even the news there in the West happened in a more significant way, and that the conclusions drawn from them were deeper. Pushkin then said in a resounding young voice: "Gentlemen, the English have landed in the north."

Everyone glanced quizzically at each other, but de Heeckeren's nephew, swarthy, nimble as a bug, ran up to the poet, leapt up, slapped him on the cheek and slipped off into the crowd. Pushkin clenched his fists, but realized that the French agent was once again deliberately provoking a scandal, and that he wanted a duel in order to kill him on the sly. No, this shall not be, thought Pushkin, the people need me, and the honor of the people is above personal honor.

But de Heeckeren's nephew flitted through the crowd, whispering something into everyone's ears. There he was next to Arakcheev, and then next to Alexander himself. And Pushkin was banned from the home of his friends Zhukovsky and Vyazemsky.

Pushkin left this stifling atmosphere and stepped out into the fresh air, and there the simple people had gathered, recognized the poet, were delighted and said:

"Master, the French will not allow us to live, the villains have taken all our money and land away. They weary us with theft and toture us with blows. The French are a plague on the Russian people."

And Pushkin answered, "Take heart, brothers. God has sent us this trial. And since he has sent it, he must believe that we can survive the trial. A great future awaits Russia, and we must be worthy of it."

"Thank you, master," answered the people.

At that moment a messenger made his way through the crowd and said that the Japanese had already landed in Vladivostok. Pushkin then made the sign of the cross over the crowd, appointed as leader his faithful companion Nikolai Chernyshevsky the Fierce, embraced him, kissed him three times, and sent him against the Japanese. But he decided to keep luring Bonaparte in to allow him to approach even closer.

Alexander Seergevich returned again to the hall. And there chaos reigned, everyone was screaming that all Russians should go to the West, to improve their stock, and only after at least two or three generations, having corrected and purged their Asiatic scourge, to return to Russia and start from scratch. In a ringing, strong voice, Pushkin said: "Gentlemen, the Japanese have landed in the East." Everyone turned toward him in incomprehension. Meanwhile, de Heeckeren's nephew ran out into the middle of the hall; he stood before the great poet, fidgety as a little devil, and under the approving roar of all of high society began to tell all sorts of obscene and totally made-up stories about the wife of the great poet, Natalia Goncharova, accompanying his tales with obscene gestures and body movements. "And, overall, all Russian women are…" he said and dropped a tremendous obscenity. Everyone laughed and applauded, even Nicholas and Benkendorf graciously bowed their heads. Pushkin understood then that he could no longer suffer these insults, not only to the honor of his wife, but that of all Russian women. Then he raised his glittering eyes to the enemy and said, "For insulting the honor of the women of my beloved land, I challenge you to a duel tomorrow at Chornaya Rechka."

De Heeckeren's nephew started quivering like an aspen leaf and fell to the floor. Then the imposing de Heeckeren himself came forth and said, smiling: "We accept your challenge." He took his collapsed nephew into his arms like a baby and carried him off. And Pushkin was banned from the home of his friends Turgenev and Tyutchev.

Pushkin left this stifling atmosphere and stepped out into the fresh air, and there the simple people had gathered, recognized the poet, were delighted, and said:

"Master, the French will not allow us to live, the villains have taken all our money and land away. They weary us with theft and toture us with blows. The French are a plague on the Russian people."

And Pushkin answered, "Take heart, brothers. God has sent us this trial. And since he has sent it, he must believe that we can survive the trial. A great future awaits Russia, and we must be worthy of it. "

"Thank you, master," answered the people.

Then a messenger made his way through the crowd and said that Bonaparte had reached Borodino, and was observing Moscow from the Poklonnaya Hill, trying to figure out how to capture the city. Then the great poet made the sign of the cross over the crowd, threw his overcoat over his shoulders in a quick movement, donned his sword, had his warhorse brought to him, and led the people to meet the treacherous enemy. When they all arrived at the field of Borodino it was already evening. Alexander Sergeyevich ordered that trenches be dug, fortifications and pillboxes put up, bridges and lines of communication be built. All night the people worked and built an impregnable line of defense. And the great poet gave instructions for where everyone should stand, which Marshal should lead which troops, where to set up the artillery batteries, where to hide in ambush, who should start and who should conclude, said that he'd be right back, and that they should start without him if necessary, and galloped off to Chornaya Rechka.

Pushkin rode to Chornaya Rechka, where de Heeckeren's nephew and his accomplices had already had an hour or two to set something up. The nephew himself was pale, weak as a lizard, swallowing pills to calm his nerves, and had put on under his shirt some sort of impenetrable armor made of a secret alloy. Pushkin looked at him with even some pity, took his revolver, and stepped away to load the gun. And at that moment, while he was loading his gun with his back to his enemies, so as not to embarrass them, a shot rang out and a bullet went right into the heart of the great poet. He fell, and de Heeckeren's nephew, running in circles like a rabbit, started to run away, along with his henchmen. "Stop!"shouted Pushkin. "Stop!" But they just fled faster into the forest. Then Pushkin, with the last of his strength, aimed and fired. Pushkin's bullet pierced de Heeckeren's nephew's steel armor and felled him on the spot. The dying poet's remaining bullets felled the collaborators of the French agent as well.

And at that moment, the Russian people, thanks to the great poet's skillful disposition of forces, routed the French at Borodino and celebrated a complete and total victory. They began to look for Pushkin, but could not find him. Only on the third day one of the rescue teams came across the still body of the great Russian poet. They picked him up, laid him on a heavy artillery carriage covered in imperial purple silk, placed a shield at his head and a sword at his feet, and, to the mournful sounds of a brass band, took him off to the field of Borodino. The troops stood in formation with their banners dropped, and with a friendly saluting volley, they laid him into the damp earth. And everyone started weeping, even the defeated Bonaparte and his generals. The body of de Heeckeren's young and dastardly nephew remained in the field, to be torn to pieces by the crows and wolves.

The poet cannot live without his people, but neither can the people live without its poet.

AND DEAD FELL
THE ENEMIES

(c. 1975-1985)

Long ago in Old Russia there lived a Great Russian writer. He was famous throughout the world, even among those who could not read Russian, even among those who could not even read at all.

He was of the noblest and purest origin. On his father's side he descended from Rurik himself, while his mother was a direct descendant of Ivan the Terrible. No surname was more famous, and no one of that family was as talented a writer as he.

The writer lived in accordance with his nobility and wealth, and the standards of his circle. He went to balls, ate in restaurants, played cards, fought duels, and wrote books. He tried everything and was lucky in everything.

Once, he went with friends and Gypsy girls to Yar, the famous restaurant outside of Moscow. Halfway there they stopped. The driver said: "Master, the axle is broken. It must be fixed." The writer got out of the carriage. For the first time in his life he found himself on foot outside his estate or the English Club. And all around him there was groaning. The peasants were slaving away in the fields, the women were harnessed to the plow, children were crying and swelling up with hunger, the emaciated livestock was wailing, and the low grain rustled sorrowfully. The writer looked all around himself, and his soul was wounded by all of the suffering.

He jumped back into the carriage and gave the order to gallop back home. His friends and the Gypsy girls were surprised, but the writer stayed silent, and merely hurried the coachman. They came clattering home. And immediately the writer sold his estate, Yasnaya Polyana, to some friend, gave away all the livestock, furniture, clothes, money and land to the poor, and headed off to the people.

He got to the people, by the Volga, and got himself hired as a barge hauler. He was of enormous stature and incredible strength, and he defended the rights of ordinary working people everywhere. The brigade where he worked got paid better and was fed better food. The writer was respected among the people, who wondered: how did such a literate and righteous man wind up among them.

The writer observed the lives of the people and realized that he could not work in all the factories, all the brigades and cooperatives, in all the planting and mowing fields at once, in order to stand up for the people's truth. He understood that only a revolution could help. He wrote the song about the petrel, proudly fluttering over the gray abyss of the sea, entirely unafraid of the storm, while all sorts of dastardly penguins and loons hid their fat bodies somewhere warmer. In this song, the great writer exposed the enemies and called on the people to rise up. The people learned about this song and rose up.

But the people failed to grip their arms firmly enough, and they were defeated.

The penguins and loons attacked the great writer, shouting: "You should not have taken up arms." The writer stood up straight and said, proudly, "We should have, but should have done so with greater courage and determination." But the people were deceived and believed the loons and penguins, and the writer began to be followed by the Third Department.

Said the writer: "Someday they will realize that I was right, that I supported them with all of my heart." Then he slipped away from the surveillance and fled to Italy and the deserted island of Capri. He built himself a little lean-to and began to live there, eating berries and mushrooms. On a small stump, which he used as a table, the writer began to create a magnificent book about the working class, to open the people's eyes to this deception.

All over the world, in every country, they heard that in Italy, on the desert island of Capri, there lived a sage who ate only berries and mushrooms, and who was scribbling away at something day and night. People began coming to him for advice. He helped the Italian railway workers to win a strike, the British to establish their *treidunions*, and the Germans to organize the Second International. And he spoke to each in that person's native language, without the slightest accent; this was his only weakness. He asked each visitor about his health, his wife and children, gave advice, taught them something and then let them go in peace. And the glory of his name spread.

And then one day, like thunder in clear skies, the great writer's book was published, the world's first book on the working class. The Russian people understood then that they had irreparably offended the great writer, and the people became agitated.

The Tsar read the book and realized that his end had come. Then he sent an agent of the Third Department to Capri. The agent came and said to the great Russian writer: "It was the Tsar himself who sent me. O writer, take on supreme authority in Russia, obey no one but the Tsar. You will make the people happy, and you will have great power." But the great Russian writer answered: "I do not want to come to the people through authority. I want them to come to me themselves, out of love." And the agent went away with nothing.

And the people grew still more agitated. Then the Tsar sent a second agent of the Third Department to Capri. The agent came and said to the great Russian writer: "It was the Tsar himself who sent me. The people are hungry. O writer, take on supreme authority in Russia, feed the people, obey no one but the Tsar." But the great Russian writer answered: "I do not want to lure the people in with bread. I want them to come to me themselves, out of love." And the agent went away with nothing.

And the people grew still more agitated. A deputation of workers came to the great writer and said: "We have offended you, but now we understand everything. Lead us, writer—we will create something unprecedented, hitherto non-existent in the world. Be our chief." And the writer answered: "Fine. Right away, just let me get my things together."

He came to Russia and led the people to storm the Winter Palace, the stronghold of autocracy. Cannons were firing all around, machine guns chattering, heavy artillery pounding, bombs exploding, hell of a pandemonium, but the writer took the Winter Palace. And—a remarkable detail—none of his people were killed or even injured.

And thus Soviet power was established. Happiness commenced: everyone walked the streets well-fed, happy, smiling. There is the writer out strolling, and everyone bows to him, gives thanks, and wishes him many years of life.

But the enemies never rested, and they sent spies disguised as doctors to the great Russian writer. These enemies of the people convinced the writer that he needed medical treatment. And the people loved the writer so much that they believed the enemy doctors. And thus they doctored the perfectly healthy great Russian writer to death.

When the people found out about it, they ripped the doctor-spies to shreds, as well as other enemies that had been discovered.

But, thanks to the death of the great Russian writer, Soviet power was only strengthened. The people realized what great happiness the writer had been preparing for them, since his enemies were so afraid of him. And so every single one of them came to support Soviet power.

Thus, with his own death, the great Russian writer felled his enemies.

THE DELEGATE FROM
VASILYEVSKY ISLAND

(c. 1975–1985)

One day, at the end of a session of the Party Congress in Zurich, everyone had departed, and only a group of comrades from the Central Committee remained. It was a bright summer day. Bright sunshine flooded the room and illuminated their young, impetuous faces.

Then Vladimir Ilyich noticed a girl in the back corner, rapidly scribbling in her notebook. She was lovely: tall, slim, enormous blue eyes, regular and soft features, a well-defined chin, and a huge reddish braid that hung to her waist.

Vladimir Ilyich asked among his comrades, and they replied that she was the delegate from Vasilyevsky Island. Lenin approached the girl, examining her with a kindly and attentive look, and said: "Our comrades on Vasilyevsky Island are not without a taste for beauty."

The girl blushed, lowered her eyes and replied: "Beauty lies in our struggle for a brighter future."

Lenin replied: "Nor do our comrades from Vasilyevsky Island lack good sense."

The girl replied: "Good sense is that which guarantees the future."

Lenin turned to Comrade Stalin and said: "Can you imagine, Joseph Vissarionovich, the kind of life we will build with youth like this!" Stalin replied: "In the Caucasus, we say that if the girl is beautiful, it brings honor to her parents, and if she is clever, it brings honor to her nation."

The girl looked down, smoothed her hair and replied: "It is the honor of my parents to have raised me to be honest and humble, and it is the honor of my nation that I was raised with a sense of truth and justice."

Vladimir Ilyich smiled and asked Stalin: "So, what do you all say in this case?" Joseph Vissarionovich smiled, sweetly crinkled his eyes and responded: "In cases like this, we in the Caucasus don't say anything—we fall in love."

At that moment Martov and Plekhanov came up from behind. Both had long sought to betroth their daughters to Lenin. They looked with disdain upon the delegate from Vasilyevsky Island and said: "Our daughters have been Party members in good standing for ten years, and we ourselves have been in the Party since our youth, and undergone penal servitude and exile, when this girl here was barely crawling on all fours under the table. And we don't even know who her parents are."

Vladimir Ilyich looked at Stalin and said: "Well, the comrades are right." Stalin smiled slyly into his mustache and said: "Let's have an examination. Whoever passes will be right."

Martov and Plekhanov sent for their daughters. They came—fat and old, with sour, dissatisfied faces.

Lenin said: "Here's the first question: Who are the Bolsheviks and who are the Mensheviks?"

The daughters of Martov and Plekhanov were unable to answer. But the girl, the delegate from Vasilyevsky Island, threw her reddish braid behind her back, directed her open gaze straight into the eyes of Vladimir Ilyich and said: "The Mensheviks are those who are greater but will be fewer, and the Bolsheviks are those who are now fewer, but who will later be greater."

All the comrades of the Central Committee marveled at her wise answer, and Vladimir Ilyich even slapped his right knee in satisfaction.

The second task was to sneak leaflets into a factory. The daughters of Martov and Plekhanov were immediately caught by the police and were only released with great difficulty. But the girl, the delegate from Vasilyevsky Island, not only snuck the leaflets into the factory, but also managed to organize a strike and lead it to a successful conclusion.

All the comrades of the Central Committee marveled at her mature work, and Vladimir Ilyich narrowed his eyes and looked at the girl in a new way.

"Well, well," said Vladimir Ilyich "Here's the last task for you. Information has to come to us that a traitor has wound up in our midst. Identify him."

No matter how hard they tried, the daughters of Martov and Plekhanov were unable to identify the traitor.

But the girl, the delegate from Vasilyevsky Island, looked into the crowd of people, and then Zinoviev came out of the crowd and said: "I can no longer bear her honest, piercing gaze. I'm the traitor." From that time on, the girl revealed many traitors in this way.

All the comrades of the Central Committee marveled at her insight, and Vladimir Ilyich said to Stalin: "What do you say to that?" Joseph Vissarionovich smiled, shook his head and replied: "I'd steal her and take her off to the Caucasus straight away, if she weren't needed for Party work here right now."

And the girl held back a smile, brushed the hair from her brow, and said: "If the Party sends me to the Caucasus, I'll go to the Caucasus."

The personal data of the girl were in order, she had good recommendations, plus the Central Committee supported her candidacy. Her name was Nadezhda Krupskaya.

From that time on, she was with Lenin everywhere. They whiled away many cold nights together in Shushenskoe. She was with him on the memorable Cruiser Aurora, when all 40 of its legendary guns smashed the Winter Palace into splinters—that bastion of autocracy. And she was at Ilyich's deathbed.

And so to them were born three sons. The first joined the peasants, the second the workers. The third joined the soldiers. The sons grew, and the first son provided ever so much food for the country, the second son gave ever so many goods to the country, and the third son guarded the country ever so vigilantly.

FOREVER LIVING

(c. 1975-1985)

It happened long ago, once upon a time.

One early June morning, on June 22, without any warning or declaration of war, a thirty-million-strong Chinese horde crossed the gray-haired waters of the Amur and treacherously attacked peaceful Soviet Siberia.

The Soviet troops courageously received the dastardly enemy's blows. Yet their forces were too unequal. Furthermore, it was spring, the roads were impassable, the great Siberian rivers Yenisei, Irtysh, Lena, and Angara were overflowing their banks, and help was prevented from arriving in time by climatic circumstances.

The Chinese surrounded the headquarters of Soviet head commander General Lazo with their thirty million and shouted: "Surrender, heroic Lazo! You alone are left!"

But Lazo just fired a long burst from his machine gun. When his ammunition ran out and Lazo realized that it was not possible to bring in any more, he threw himself into the waters of the Amur and swam off. The Chinese set their machine guns and heavy artillery up on the high banks of the Amur River and started shooting at Lazo, but they were not accurate, sometimes undershooting and sometimes overshooting. It was already midday when a stray bullet hit Lazo in the head. Wounded, he was taken captive.

He stood there, huge and blond, his head covered in blood, his eyes sparkling, while little, yellow, nimble Chinese were running all around him. All thirty million of them surrounded him, fending him off with their bayonets. And they shouted: "Come join us, heroic Lazo. We'll get rich! Reject the Moscow revisionists!"

Lazo asked them calmly: "And whose side is Lenin on?"

"Moscow's, Moscow's!" squeaked the Chinese.

"So I am on Moscow's side, too," Lazo's thundering voice drowned out their twittering.

The Chinese jumped up and down angrily, their faces twisted, spattering saliva.

"We'll devise a terrible death for you, heroic Lazo," they hiss.

But Lazo stood still as a statue, with only his eyes burning with life.

A terrible winter was underway. Trees shattered from the cold, birds froze as they flew, without even spreading their wings, all the beasts of the forest fled toward the Urals, toward Soviet Russia.

The Chinese stripped Lazo naked, took him out into the cold and hosed him down with water. About a thousand of the Chinese pouring water on Lazo had already frozen, just like the birds, but Lazo just stood there, life still burning in his eyes. And the most incredible thing was—the snow beneath his feet began to melt and the grass to peek forth.

The Chinese were frightened, their teeth started chattering. They ran around him, threw their heads back and shouted: "Why, heroic Lazo, why won't you die?"

And Lazo replied, "All of my life is in Lenin!"

Then the Chinese locked him in a cell and sent an agent to Moscow to kill Lenin. The agent pretended to be a Chinese trader from Kitaigorod, and got through the first checkpoint outside Moscow. He wanted to get into the ancient Kremlin, but a vigilant soldier of the Kremlin guard detained him at the second checkpoint. Lenin later personally awarded this vigilant soldier from the second checkpoint of the Kremlin guard the Hero's Star, while the soldiers from the first checkpoint around Moscow were severely punished.

When the Chinese learned about the death of their agent, they came running to Lazo, sputtering saliva, shouting at him: "Beware, heroic Lazo, we'll devise a terrible death for you!" And Lazo stood there, his eyes glowering down at them.

Then the Chinese drove up a locomotive and fired up the furnace so hot that the whole train car turned pink and shivered from the heat. The Chinese threw a test piece of heat-resistant metal into the furnace, and within a moment it was transformed into a drop of liquid. Then the Chinese shoved Lazo into the furnace, and stood around in a circle, rubbing their little hands, and stamping their feet with joy.

But, after only a few moments, the Chinese could see Lazo walking back and forth in the furnace, unharmed, bending to pick something up and singing "The Internationale." And it was as though there was someone else there with him, singing along with him.

The Chinese were frightened, their teeth started chattering. They removed Lazo from the furnace and shouted at him: "Why, heroic Lazo, why won't you die?" Lazo answered them from on high: "My whole life is in Lenin!"

Then the Chinese locked him in a cell, and sent an agent to Moscow to kill Lenin. The agent pretended to be a Chinese trader from Kitaigorod, and got through the first checkpoint around Moscow. Then the agent pretended to be a soldier from the Eighth Liberation Army of China led by Comrade Mao Zedong, got through the second checkpoint of the Kremlin guard, and got into the ancient Kremlin. He wanted to get into Lenin's office, but a vigilant bodyguard of the third checkpoint detained him. Lenin personally awarded the vigilant soldier from the third checkpoint the Hero's Star, while the soldiers of the first checkpoint around Moscow, and the second checkpoint of the Kremlin guard, were severely punished.

When the Chinese learned about the death of their agent, they came running to Lazo, bouncing with anger and making little fists, and shouted at him: "Beware, heroic Lazo, we'll devise a terrible death for you!" And Lazo's eyes glowered down at them.

Then the Chinese built an enormous gallows and greased the rope with a special Chinese grease. They put the rope around Lazo's neck and pulled the platform from under his feet. They stood around in a circle giggling and rubbing their little hands with pleasure. But it was as if someone had lifted up Lazo, the noose was not tightening around him, and he seemed to soar. He even spread wide his enormous arms, spread his enormous legs and with his head included made the image of a gigantic five-pointed star hanging high.

The Chinese were frightened, their teeth started chattering. As they removed him from the noose they shouted at him: "Why, heroic Lazo, why don't you die?"

Lazo answered them from on high: "My whole life is in Lenin!"

Then the Chinese locked him in a cell, and sent an agent to Moscow to kill Lenin. The agent pretended to be a Chinese trader from Kitai-gorod and got through the first checkpoint around Moscow. Then the agent pretended to be a soldier from the Eighth Liberation Army of China led by Comrade Mao Zedong, and got through the second checkpoint of the Kremlin guards, and got into the ancient Kremlin. Next he pretended to be a comrade from the Comintern and got through the third personal security checkpoint into Lenin's office. Lenin saw a comrade from the Comintern, rose, smiled kindly and invited him to have a seat. The agent sat facing Lenin in a huge armchair, squeezing the knife in his pocket. Lenin asked him with concern: "How goes it with the red proletariat in China?" The agent snatched his knife and plunged it straight into Lenin's heart. They caught him on the spot. The soldiers of the first checkpoint around Moscow, the second checkpoint at the Kremlin, and the bodyguard at the third checkpoint were all severely punished.

When the Chinese learned of the death of Lenin, they rejoiced and ran to Lazo, bouncing with joy as they ran, leaping over each other's heads, and shouted: "Well, heroic Lazo, we've devised a terrible death for you!" They ran up to Lazo, and he was lying there, huge, the entire length of the cell, but dead, with his eyes gazing at the blue sky. And carved on his chest was: "Lenin shall live forever!"

The Chinese were frightened, their teeth started chattering. They did not know what to do. And at that time the Soviet forces approached and, with their Katyusha heavy artillery, cruisers, and battleships, cut off the Chinese from retreated through the waters of the gray-haired Amur River, and burned up all thirty million Chinese on the spot.

Lazo was buried with military honors, and a monument was erected to him. And they erected a monument to Lenin next to it. And every time Lazo looks at Lenin, it's as if life flickers in his copper gaze.

THE BATTLE ACROSS THE OCEAN

THE OCEAN

(c. 1975–1985)

Once upon a time Nixon, the American President, and Comrade Khrushchev, the First Secretary of the Communist Party and Chairman of the Council of Ministers of the USSR, got into an argument over who was better at hockey. The American President Nixon said, "How do you Soviets think you can compete with us. Our players are all two meters tall. They don't work, they don't study, they spend their whole lives playing hockey. In a word, they're professionals. The key ones are: Phil Esposito, Mister Armored Tank; Hardy Howe, Mister Big Elbows; and Bobby Hull, Mister Terrifying Gun. We beat the Czechs, beat the Swedes, the Germans and we will beat you Soviets." The American President Nixon summoned Mister Armored Tank Phil Esposito; Mister Big Elbows Hardy Howe; Mister Terrifying Gun Bobby Hull. They came into his office, each taller than two meters, even without their padded uniforms they could barely squeeze through the door; their teeth were iron and they were always chewing something. Comrade Khrushchev, First Secretary of the CPSU Central Committee and Chairman of the Council of Ministers of the USSR, grew sad, while Nixon, the American President, laughed.

First Secretary of the CPSU Central Committee and Chairman of the Council of Ministers of the USSR Comrade Khrushchev flew to Moscow, and Politburo Member and Party Comrade Shelepin met him at the Vnukovo airport. As he met him, he asked, "What has made you so sad?" First Secretary of the CPSU Central Committee and Chairman of the Council of Ministers of the USSR Comrade Khrushchev replied: "The American President Nixon and I got into an argument about whose hockey was better. And it does appear that they are better. All their players are two-meter-tall professionals. And the most important ones are Mister Armored Tank Phil Esposito; Mister Big Elbows Hardy Howe; and Mister Terrifying Gun Bobby Hull. We really can't compete with them." Member of the Politburo Comrade Shelepin fell into thought and replied: "It is not fit for the Americans to triumph over Soviets. Go, get some sleep, and I'll think of something."

Politburo Member Comrade Shelepin gathered together his deputies, aides and assistants and said: "We are not used to playing hockey, but it would not be fit for the Americans to triumph over the Russians." And he gave them one day's time to find volunteers to fight the Americans. That very night, a list lay on the desk of Comrade Khrushchev, First Secretary of the CPSU Central Committee and Chairman of the Council of Ministers. Here it is: Captain Boris Mikhailov; Komsomol Organizer Vladimir Petrov; Hockey Magician Valery Kharlamov; Alexander "The Magnificent" Yakushev; the Unbending Vladimir Shadrin; Five-Striker Vyacheslav Starshinov; the Attack-Leader Boris Mayorov; the Impenetrable Vladimir Lutchenko; Ice Guard Alexander Gusev; "Russian Ivan" Valery Vasiliev; "Ivan the Terrible" Alexander Ragulin; and Komsomol Central Committee Member Vladislav Tretiak. All of them left their studies at institutions of higher education, their home factories, their collective or state farms, and said goodbye to their wives, kissed their little kiddies, and flew away to America.

The Soviet hockey players landed in the enemy camp. They went out onto the ice. The Americans, 50 of them, all huge, in glittering helmets, were banging their hockey sticks on the ice. And the Americans said: "Hey, Russkies, you've come to lose?" And our guys replied: "One wins through deeds, not through words." The Americans said: "Our deeds are in our sticks." And the Soviets answered: "Our deeds are in our hearts." And so the match began. Our guys each got past 5 or 6 opponents to toss the puck through the goalposts. The Americans tried to trip them up behind the ref's back, beating and murdering our fellas. Mister Armored Tank Phil Esposito made the biggest effort. And the refs, bribed by the Americans, pretended not to notice. Six Soviet players were carried off the field. But the victory was ours, 10:0. Score by period: first period—5:0, second period—3:0, third period—2:0. Goals were scored by the Magnificent Alexander Yakushev (4), Hockey Magician Valery Kharlamov (3), Five-Striker Vyacheslav Starshinov (2), Komsomol organizer Vladimir Petrov (1). And there were many more goals that the refs wouldn't count.

Our players returned to the hotel, but Captain Boris Mikhailov, Unbending Vladimir Shadrin, Ice Guard Alexander Gusev and Attack-Leader Boris Mayorov passed away without recovering consciousness. Meanwhile, Hockey Magician Valeri Kharlamov and Impenetrable Vladimir Lutchenko were down with serious injuries. The Soviet hockey players buried their companions and gathered for a meeting. In the enemy camp there was great celebration, the Americans were drinking whiskey and shouting: "Hey, Soviets, tomorrow we'll show you!" Politburo member Comrade Shelepin rose up and said: "It would not be fit for the Americans to triumph over the Soviets. Tomorrow we must win." They determined that each would play for themselves and for their fallen comrades.

They went out for the second match. The Americans, 50 of them, all huge, in glittering helmets, were banging their hockey sticks on the ice. And the Americans said: "Hey, Russkies, you've come to lose?" And our guys replied, "One wins through deeds, not through words." The Americans said: "Our deeds are in our sticks." And the Soviets answered: "Our deeds are in our hearts." And so the match began. Our guys each got past 7 or 8 opponents, to toss the puck through the goalposts. The Americans tried to trip them up behind the ref's back, beating and murdering our fellas. Mister Big Elbows Hardy Howe made the biggest effort. And the refs, bribed by the Americans, pretended not to notice. Six Soviet players were carried off the field. But victory was ours: 8:3. Score by period: First period—3:0, Second period—2:1, Third period—3:2. Goals scored: Alexander "The Magnificent" Yakushev (4), Hockey Magician Valery Kharlamov (3), Five-Striker Vyacheslav Starshinov (1). And there were many more goals that the ref wouldn't count.

Our players returned to the hotel, but Komsomol Organizer Vladimir Petrov, Five-Striker Vyacheslav Starshinov, Impenetrable Vladimir Lutchenko, and "Russian Ivan" Valery Vasiliev had all passed away without regaining consciousness. Likewise, Alexander "the Magnificent" Yakushev and "Ivan the Terrible" Alexander Ragulin were laid up with severe injuries. The Soviet hockey players buried their comrades and gathered for a meeting. And in the enemy camp there was great celebration, the Americans were drinking whiskey and shouting: "Hey, Soviets, tomorrow we'll show you!" Politburo member Comrade Shelepin arose and said: "It would not be fit for the Americans to triumph over the Soviets. Tomorrow we must win." And they determined that each would play for themselves and for their fallen comrades.

They went out for the third match. The Americans, 50 of them, all huge, their helmets glittering, were knocking their sticks against the ice. And the Americans said: "Hey, Russkies, did you come here to lose?" And our guys replied, "We'll win, not with words but with deeds." The Americans said: "Our deeds are in our sticks." And the Soviets answered: "Our deeds are in our hearts." And so the match began. Our guys each got past 7 or 8 opponents, to toss the puck through the goalposts. The Americans tried to trip them up behind the ref's back, beating and murdering our fellas. Mister Terrifying Gun Bobby Hull made the biggest effort. And the ref, bribed by the Americans, pretended not to notice. Already three Soviet hockey players had been carried off the field, leaving only one, Komsomol Central Committee member Vladislav Tretiak, wounded all over but whispering: "They shall not pass, they shall not pass!" Only three seconds remained in the match. Then two seconds. Then one second. Then the bell. Komsomol Central Committee member Vladislav Tretiak fell to the ice covered in blood, but the victory remained ours: 4:3. The score by periods: first period—1:0, second period—1:1, third period—2:2. Goals scored: Alexander "the Magnificent" Yakushev (4). And there were many more goals the ref wouldn't count.

Politburo member Comrade Shelepin lifted up Komsomol Central Committee member Vladislav Tretiak, and even the enemies were surprised, removed their hats and said: "We've been playing hockey for so many years, but this is the first time we've seen anything like this." The Politburo member and Komsomol Central Committee member Vladislav Tretiak got on an airplane and flew to Moscow. And at the Vnukovo airport they were met by the people, their families, women, and children with flowers. Komsomol Central Committee member Vladislav Tretiak came out of the plane, walked straight across the red carpet to First Secretary of the CPSU Central Committee and Chairman of the Council of Ministers of USSR Comrade Khrushchev and said: "Comrade First Secretary of the CPSU Central Committee and Chairman of the Council of Ministers of the USSR, the task laid upon me by the Motherland has been completed." He said it, and dropped dead.

And ever since then, in America they no longer play hockey.

THE AWESOME
STONE AVENGER

(c. 1975–1985)

In a little tiny village in the remote Siberian taiga, not too far from the town of Simbirsk, a certain boy was born. His father was a true native Russian, though a strange person: wherever he held out his hand, there grew a tree; wherever he glanced, a log cabin would go up in flames; whoever he might say an unkind word to, that person would die.

No one remembered anything about the boy's mother. It was said that she had appeared with some dark-skinned people. Their appearance was marvelous and their speech made no sense, and they were always hurrying somewhere. Among them was only one woman; she gave birth to the boy and departed with the dark-skinned people, maybe to the East, maybe to the West... The boy grew up to resemble his father—extremely tall and fair-haired—and only his black eyes came from his mother. And they were so black that even when he was a child no one could withstand his gaze. And whoever persisted would wander around for a few days afterward in a kind of daze. The boy's name was Evgeny Vuchetich.

And it was revealed that he had an extraordinary gift: he could take a stone into his hands, and it would become a beast, as if alive. He could take a piece of wood in his hands—and it would become a face, as if alive. He could take clay into his hands, and it would become a person, as if alive. Experts predicted a great future for him. However, when he reached the age of 18, something happened to him. He wanted to sculpt a beautiful woman... but his strength left him, his hands hung limp. He wanted to carve a beautiful torso... but his hands could not lift the chisel, even though they had been dragging heavy logs moments before. He wanted to carve a lovely figure… but the chisel fell from his hands and cut his finger, and it bled.

So Vuchetich left home and did not come back. He left for the big city and began working on a lathe at the factory. He was a good worker, a shock-worker, he received certificates, and quite a few times was presented with awards. It seemed like he had forgotten all about his secret gift. Only sometimes, during breaks or on weekends, he would disappear to no one knew where. He would return silent, his face dark. All around him was happiness and peace, but he seemed to have a premonition of something.

The Great Patriotic War broke out. The Germans attacked the Soviet Union and immediately began to conquer it. Nothing could stop them. They moved like an avalanche and the earth buzzed with German tanks, guns, and boots. Vuchetich decided to volunteer for the front. He resigned from his job, went back home to get his things together, and unexpectedly fell asleep before bedtime. He dreamed of boundless snowfields, but then far off in the distance a black dot appeared, it grew and grew, and he heard a metallic clatter—and there was Peter the Great, all in black, on a black horse, in black radiance. He raised his hand and said: "Listen to me. Go to Stalingrad." He said this and once again turned into a dot in the endless expanse of snow. And so Vuchetich went to Stalingrad.

They enemy had already captured the whole country, only Stalingrad was left. The enemy had driven all the troops to the city and was bombarding it daily. Not a single house was left standing. Vuchetich came to Stalingrad, and immediately went to the Malakoff burial mound. He lifted a huge stone, placed it on the center of the mound and began to work from morning to night, constructing a stone statue. People began to help him carry stones. Then the District, City, and Regional Party Committees sent special units to help him. Soon there were three million people working under Vuchetich. The country faced difficulties, without sufficient manpower, equipment or food. But for Vuchetich, the country spared nothing.

And there began to rise a huge statue of Stalin, encircled by an army of stone. Every day, from morning to night, the Germans fired their guns at Stalingrad, bombed it from their planes, doused it with napalm. Everything in the city was destroyed, but strangely, not a single bullet, shell, or bomb fell on the Malakoff mound. No one was killed there, none were injured, nor even shell-shocked.

Vuchetich was already done with the boots and an overcoat that hung close to the floor. He made the seams and folds, and they stood there as if alive. The Germans laughed and shouted: "Hey, Stalin! Come on, smash us!" But in answer, the statue only swayed.

The Germans were already close, they had occupied all of Stalingrad. For the second month running Vuchetich was working from morning till night, hauling and chopping stone. The statue had already risen waist-high. He had made sleeves, the belt, the strap, pockets, and they all stood there as if alive. The Germans laughed and shouted: "Hey, Stalin! Come on, smash us!" But in answer, the statue only swayed.

The Germans had surrounded the Malakoff mound, and there were barely any defenders left. At this point the statue was done up to the shoulders. Vuchetich had carved in the collar, the epaulettes, and the polished medals, and they all stood there as if alive. And the stone army had grown into an endless host. The Germans laughed and shouted: "Hey, Stalin! Come on, smash us!" But in answer, the statue only swayed.

On the final night of the third month, Vuchetich finished his work. His three million assistants fell asleep right at the feet of the statue as the moon rose. Vuchetich climbed up the wooden scaffolding to the head of Stalin. So high up it was lost in the clouds. Vuchetich ran his hands across the mustache, the cheeks, the eyes, and suddenly a black fire blazed forth in the pupils of the statue. Vuchetich was frightened. He dropped down to the statue's feet, fell to his knees and said: "Here I am. I've done everything I can! I can do no more."

Just then there was a thunderclap and the wooden scaffolding collapsed. Far behind the front lines, in the German rear, a fire broke out. The earth shook, and a whirlwind swept from East to West. The Germans jumped up and screamed: "Stalin is coming!" They rushed to escape, illuminated by some sort of harsh light. And Stalin was on the move with his stone army. Wherever his feet came down lay crushed German divisions; wherever his hands passed, ruined cities lay smoking; wherever his gaze fell, there lay burnt-out tanks, planes, and artillery.

And he drove the Germans to Berlin. He took Berlin—and disappeared. He was never seen again anywhere, but to this day, on the territory of Poland and Germany, Czechoslovakia and Bulgaria, Romania and Albania people still find huge stones. They say that they are the warriors of his victorious army.

But Vuchetich and his three million assistants were killed by the first retaliatory German salvo. And so, to this day, no one anywhere in the world can create anything that can compare with it.

THE TALE OF ALEXEYEV, THRICE HERO OF THE SOVIET UNION

(c. 1975–1985)

1.

A long time ago there lived in Moscow a prominent worker of one of the Ministries by the name of Alexeyev. He was a decorated person and a member of the Party since 1905. The leaders trusted him with tasks of the most critical significance, and he carried them out honorably. His wife was also an honorable woman and a Party member. They lived with dignity, only they had no child. They sought out the most cutting-edge medical treatments, and in the end, a son was born to them.

2.

He grew up, did not succumb to harmful outside influences and began to lead a disorderly way of life. He even planned to try out for an operetta theater, as he displayed some talent in this area. Then they found him an appropriate bride, who was also the daughter of senior officials.

3.

The wedding feast was underway, with the guests of honor giving advice to the newlyweds. Finally, it was time to go to the marriage bed. He wanted to give a farewell toast, but when he unwrapped the bottle, a newspaper fell to the floor. He picked up the newspaper and saw an article by Lenin about the famine in Siberia. He read the burning lines attentively and felt his heart turn over in his chest. "I have led my whole life incorrectly," he whispered, and without even entering the bedroom, he quietly left the house. He got on the first train and went to Siberia. When he was found to be missing, the bride wept and said: "I shall remain single." His mother died of grief. And the father began to come home from work later and later.

4.

Alexeyev arrived in Siberia and began looking for the most difficult place. He was tossed out by the narrow gauge railway. In the dead of winter, without boots, without a shovel, he dug the earth with his bare hands and fought off bandits. Then, one time, everyone was killed, and he alone managed to escape. He crawled through the taiga for ten days, biting off bits of his belt. He was found and rescued by Nanai people sympathetic to the Soviets. His frostbitten feet had to be amputated. Alexeyev himself asked them to do the surgery without anesthesia. All that came out of his pale lips was: "You lie, you won't do it." The doctors were astonished at such courage and said: "After so many years in medicine, this is the first time we have seen anything like this." They made him prosthetics, and after only one month, he was dancing the mazurka. No one would ever have guessed what had happened, except that his hair had prematurely turned gray.

5.

The Great Patriotic War broke out. Alexeyev hid from the doctors that he did not have real legs, only prosthetics, and went to the front line. And he ended up in the division his father, now a General, commanded, and where his wife was a doctor in the hospital. The country was having a hard time. The enemy, which outnumbered them, had reached the capital and was pummeling it with its tanks. And this was the point where Alexeyev stood his ground. For three days he held back the enemy tanks, until reinforcements arrived. They brought him to the hospital gravely wounded. They put him on the operating table and his wife took up the scalpel. Alexeyev himself asked them to do the surgery without anesthesia. All that came out of his pale lips was: "You lie, you won't do it." The doctors marveled at such courage and said: "After so many years in medicine, this is the first time we have seen anything like this." The General himself, his father, came, but did not recognize his son, and he said: "You're a hero, and deserve special treatment." Alexeyev responded: "If I am a hero and deserve special treatment, Comrade General, then release me back to the front." Since he had a head wound, he had managed to hide from doctors that he did not have real legs, only prosthetics, and he went back to the front. Right then his Hero's Star medal arrived and they wanted to award it to him; they searched for him but could not find him.

6.

The country began to overcome the enemy and beat him back to his own territory. And Alexeyev moved onto enemy territory. One day, there was a battle for the German city Karl Marx Stadt. Surrounded by exploding bombs, Alexeyev noticed a little German girl in a white dress on the dusty pavement. Then Alexeyev crawled over and, shielding her with his heart, carried her out of the fire. They brought him to the hospital gravely wounded. They put him on the operating table and his wife took up the scalpel. Alexeyev himself asked them to do the surgery without anesthesia. All that came out of his pale lips was: "You lie, you won't do it." The doctors marveled at such courage and said: "After so many years in medicine, this is the first time we have seen anything like this." The General himself, his father, came, but did not recognize his son, and he said: "You're a hero, and deserve special treatment." Alexeyev responded: "If I am a hero and deserve special treatment, Comrade General, then release me back to the front." Since he was wounded in the hand, he had managed to hide from doctors that he did not have real legs, only prosthetics, and he went back to the front. Right then his second Heroic Star medal arrived and they wanted to award it to him; they searched but could not find him.

7.

The Soviet troops drove the enemy all the way to their lair, but still could not take the last bastion. In this place the enemy had a huge, terrifying pillbox that wouldn't let anyone pass. Alexeyev then jumped up and shouted "Hurrah!" in a thundering voice, ran up to the pillbox and shielded it with his heart. Our troops took Berlin, and Alexeyev was taken to the hospital gravely wounded. They put him on the operating table and his wife took up the scalpel. Alexeyev himself asked them to do the surgery without anesthesia. All that came out of his pale lips was: "You lie, you won't do it." The doctors marveled at such courage and said: "After so many years in medicine, this is the first time we have seen anything like this." The General himself, his father, who was already a Marshal, came, but did not recognize his son, and he said: "You're a hero, and deserve special treatment." Said Alexeyev: "If I am a hero and deserve special treatment, Comrade Marshal, then give me a piece of paper." They gave him a piece of paper, and on it he wrote down the story of his life in its entirety. When they came to give him an injection, he was already dead, but his face was shining. His wife read the note and began to sob. The Marshal put his hand on her shoulder and said, "You were the wife of a missing person, and now you've became the widow of a hero. You should be proud. I was the father of a missing person, and now have become a hero's father. We will avenge you, my son."

8.

Many Generals and Marshals came, and they personally carried the coffin of Comrade Alexeyev. To the sounds of artillery fire, the Marshals and Generals lowered the thrice Hero of the Soviet Union into the damp earth and buried him.

And in Berlin there stands to this day a bronze Alexeyev, holding a bronze sword in his right hand, and in his left—a little bronze German girl.

MY RUSSIA

(1990)

Advisory Note

My Russia, in the sense of belonging to her, but also in the sense of my personal perception of her, like, say: My Pushkin! My Lenin!

But is there anything particularly exceptional in my notion of Russia? No, nothing.

Perhaps, only the faint cold shiver from her cool hands reaching for me by night in an alien land. Her hands reach closer, closer—perhaps to embrace me, or perhaps (again, at a distance, and in night's delirium what doesn't one imagine!) to seize me by the throat. Well, and what of it? It's her right! And I would never deny being subject to her laws or desires. That's just how it is.

1.

I remember that day of Russia
It was May. In the garden lilacs blossomed
And the air, unbearably blue,
Waltzed above the spirit of the villages
And towards evening in the fields indistinct
And hazy
A distant spark glimmered
And I, like a little beast
A fluffy one
Lost myself in the vast folds of
Soviet-Russian reality
Circa 1947-50

2.

Do you recall that place?—you don't remember?
Where I was young, where I was fresh
And the radio sang loudly as it played
Of the accordion gone astray

And at the threshold of the evening
Looking out upon our lives
It whispered: you just wait a little

And Communism, Communism will come—
But I, I was already drunk
On different poisons, the dream adjusted
Oh why, oh why, my dear Just God
Why did I turn out to be right!
And now I'm already old
And you too, Russia, disillusioned
And there's still no Communism

3.

I remember, it was early autumn
A barely noteworthy arrival
When, upon the river, a steamship
Suddenly leapt up, while sadly
Raising up its only horn
The real live unicorn in the forest
Answered it

4.

He says to me: but in Russia
I, a murderer and villain
Might be pardoned all the same
Since the higher truths of life
Are something that I understand
Though I'm a murderer and villain
Yes, I say, among the people
Of Russia
That's appreciated

5.

One time we were going somewhere at night
When suddenly from somewhere a horror came out
A strange, incomprehensible, absolute horror
Its voice did tickle us, reedy and pig-like
Within it twittered our old Russian fables
Oh, those dark fables, mysterious as whirlpools
O Lord! Lord, we are ready to receive the enemy
Look, look Lord, we're as ready as snow
O Lord, here we are, Lord, we are prepared
O Lord

6.

When the heavens' living masturbation
Amazes Russia with its snow-white marvel
And all is white! white on white! then—bang and
So what does she birth in response
Our Russia?
In gratitude, so to speak!
Well, she gives birth to hell knows what
Son of a bitch

7.

When the patriots like storm clouds
Come marching from the East toward Moscow
Who could be stronger? Who's stronger is the one
Who will take that very same Moscow
And carry her like two hundred versts away
Or like five thousand versts
And then bring her back, and then again
But if she still stands in the same place
Then they are right—the patriots!—this is the advantage
    of passion in the face of indefinite positions

8.

I remember in a field near Orlov
An evil force was wandering
Mowed down everything it passed
Or simply plopped into houses
In the form of a little old man
It'd sit down, lifting up its skirts
Working the simpleton angle:
What's that? Huh? You don't like it? But our guys
The Orlovites, that is
They like it

9.

When the elephants of another world
Like black, bubbling Narzan water
From some funereal banquet
Come rolling by—I, like some
Disheveled Tarzan
Will question them, somewhat disheveled:
Where ya from, fellas? From Russia
Maybe?
No?

10.

A song is winging above poor Moscow
Above this starving Moscow of mine
Shuddering, I gaze, I do not hide
The Polovtsian dancing of worms

A pale angel takes transparent fingers
And pulls them out one by one
O Lord, how much time will this take
Even a simple mind
Cannot take it

11.

Direct correlations are severed
And the dream of the people's despair
Once again as in bygone years
Steps out, like Lermontov, onto the balcony

Opens wide prophetic eyes
And flies out above the womanly land
Like a little girl wetting her dress
With uncontrollable, internal
Blood
Her own

12.

I love the groves outside of Moscow
You love my groves?
I love them, I do!
The faint smell of pond above the pond!
You love that too?
Yes, yes!
The faint smell of pond above the pond?
I love it, I do!
The faint smell of pond above the pond
And the bloody headlong flourish—
Can you really love that too?
I do, I love it!
Even the All-Union, for instance,
Significance
Of each new maniac of yours
Brought here by autumn and disappearing in the winter!
You love that?
I do!

13.

Sigh, it isn't easy being honest
When you are so completely
Cellular—
One cell kills
Like the Communist Youth League
Another pours out tears
Like a Christian
And the third loves them
Both
And wanders lonely
In the heavens

14.

I went out to walk in the garden
But nothing came of it
I went out and again
It didn't work
Coming out into the garden
I screamed: Holy Mother!
Take me, take me out into the garden
Lead me

15.

Let me go, o portly monster
Into the spaces of my Russia
You shut both your tired
Eyes, but like a sorcerer
Pre-celestial
With your third never-fading blue eye
You tell me, staring into space
Gone mad:

Here it is—your death and Russia
So where on earth would I send you out,
Lonely one, to be dishonored

16.

I had a dream: at first all was
Like it always is, and then I died
Or it died, and all went drifting
All became wild, insane
That is, it seemed like pure mania
And, gathering my strength, recalled:
Hey, I fell asleep while out in Germany
But then I've woken up in Russia
And I compelled myself with insane force
To once again in Germany
Wake up
For now

17.

There are women, raw to their native land
When they go out
High-tension lines are moved to tears
By that superconductivity, when
Everything goes back into the earth for all eternity
Through them
These are the ones that makes it Russia
These women

18.

Now let's talk about the mice
Of which Russia has a billion

Or maybe it's already more than
A billion—but, quiet now!
She comes out alone, the mouse
And you look right into her face
Also alone

19.

When a little bitty kid
Is carried in living hands
It really doesn't take much
To make him droop and fade
From the superabundance of life itself sometimes
But there's a special fear
For the firstborn, the son
And thus Russia
Soviet Russia
The tenderest ever
Could have done me in—but I didn't fade
I turned out to be alive in my own right

20.

I remember the garden—happiness reigned there
The air there hung like Saint Aurelius
Of the Sarmatians
It hung
And everyone spoke in verse
Entirely without my participation
And all of it in insane force
Hung there—apparently Russia
Is what that was

21.

That morning we went out, it was near evening
Suddenly we smelled something damp and hot
And fresh-tilled, clean, and ovine
But also insanely wolf-like and dog-like at the same time
And we smelled burning wool—
In that corner, Russia was dying
In the feminine sense, so that at the passing
Of two eons she was supposed to birth
A son
At first no bigger than a dot, undetectable

22.

Spring in Russia. The sticky leaves
Everywhere sweet vodka
Sparkling
On every little mouse and bleak-fish
There's a tiny little star
A red one
And someone whispers, full of tenderness:
Touch, o touch my nether regions!
I am, I am!
O-o-ooooo!

23.

In Russia, I remember, at the ends of earth
Turgenev-style girls were blossoming
If you look closely, they keep blossoming
And they sing their village songs
If you reach out, they blossom redder
And run, run along the linden lane
They capture, say, Schelling, and then

Go dancing their national circle dance with him
While looking back at me

24.

For a brief interval of time
I was famous in my country
When, with my immortal name
On their lips
Girls came to me
And said: bright falcon!
Take us, lead us! And it was clear to me
That I, once again, was mortal

25.

In the evening sky the dawn burns away
It claws at the heart with its reds and its lilacs
The twilight is playing with a feminine tree
Its trunk has been twisted so marvelously

Somehow in all this one feels something
Like a supplication or just China
Something that will save us, something native
Only the answer comes: Get lost!
We hear it

26.

I sleep above Russia and still I simply cannot
Fall asleep, and like an angel of the covenant
Dividing me, this was revealed to me:
Freedom's free spine by freedom is
Broken for sure

27.

Oh my dear, in Russia, in summer
The mushrooms and berries—I have not the strength!
Yes, dear girl, but epaulets
Of the German armed forces
Are on my shoulders!

But, my dear, you see the sphere
The metaphysical one above us?
It hangs there. Thus the Russian soul
And the gloomy German genius
Did converse

28.

The gloom of an autumn day
Drizzle slapping on the roof
O Lord, I have
Nothing, not even a little mouse

I destroyed and killed them all
Crazed, amid Soviet life
Itself quite crazy
In an amulet I managed to sew up
The little slender children's bones
Also crazy

29.

To slog along in felt boots, leaden
Through Syktyvkar and swaying already
From weakness, to come suddenly
Upon a memorial and: "Doctor Goebbels"
To read the inscription

And exclaim most mournfully: My God!
In its hungering spiritual thirst
This world is unforgivably wide
I would narrow it! It can't be narrowed

30.

I will return soon to my Russia
Where everyone's been ruined by something
Historically
But I, but I will not contribute
Even though I have been asked to
Life itself asked me
But no, no, I will not contribute
It's not my job to execute by firing squad unhappy souls
   in prisons of morality

31.

I see Moscow in my mind
As capital city of the Kolyma region
When in a roadside little wood
Like a young girl who wipes away
A tear unseen by the world
With an embroidered kerchief
While pulverizing
A northern dragonfly
So pensively between her fingers

EQUILIBRIUM

(1997)

Advisory Note

One might think that a preordained harmony always underlies everything, an equilibrium implied by the space of this harmony. Here, it seems, everything has collapsed, disintegrated into tiny pieces that are incompatible and mutually antagonistic. It seems that from now on we are to exist within the bounds of some unnatural, badly-conceived, wildly positive disjunctive synthesis, having locked jaws with one another. But no, if you look closely, everyone is just being kept at the necessary cheerful distance from each other (and, occasionally, in frightening—oft necessary—mutually devastating proximity) by the fingers of this very harmony, which cannot be grasped by habitual hands fumbling in habitual places. One must look simply and honestly, not mechanically relying on an established, once-and-for-all process, apparently (to some people's juvenile delight) oriented toward self-destruction.

In parallel with this instance there is something other—and thus is equilibrium maintained.

At some station or other, say Verbilki, a kind old lady in a long cape-like coat, felt boots, and a headscarf, holding a little basket, gets on the train going towards Moscow, and at the same time an old woman just like her, with the same sort of felt boots, coat, and little basket, gets on a Moscow train going towards Verbilki—and thus is equilibrium maintained.

Here a man is being brutally murdered, and at the same moment, via a difficult labor, a child is born—thus equilibrium is maintained.

Here 20 or 30 people are being murdered, and at that moment a child is born, but an outstanding one—thus equilibrium is maintained.

Here 300 people are murdered, and in response a child is born, a genius—so equilibrium is maintained.

Here tremendous piles of humans and animals are killed, there is pestilence and famine, death and destruction, but in response a prophet is born, bringing a grandiose message of salvation—thus equilibrium is maintained.

Or, something else entirely: In Paris they speak wise and powerful words, while in Saransk spring comes early and the potatoes are planted two weeks earlier than usual—so equilibrium is maintained.

Or, there's an angel flying over the Sahara, and in response there are serious changes in the structure of language-generation among teeny-tiny scaly creatures—so equilibrium is maintained.

And finally, for example, with my left hand I tear out a tuft of hair from above my left ear and at the same time, with my right hand, I completely break off the sixth toe from my right foot—thus equilibrium is maintained.

UNBELIEVABLE STORIES

(1998)

Advisory Note

Truly, we are surrounded by the most unbelievable stories of salvation, healing, and so forth. Of countless miraculous sorceresses, healers, yogis, and faith-healers who turn back the whole causal destructive process such that one no longer wishes to simply believe in the boring and disgusting natural course of events. But then you just have to. Although it is unbelievable, alas, it is far more common and compulsory.

A completely unfathomable story: A child falls from the fourteenth floor and dies rather than survives, as was expected.

Or another other totally unbelievable story: A man was comatose for two months, but did not recover, as was expected, and died instead. Really, rather unbelievable.

And this story is no less peculiar: A man falls into the cage of a predatory beast, and says some magical words, but against all expectations is eaten down to the bones.

Or the one about how two people fell out of an airplane without parachutes and, against all expectations, fell to their deaths, although many justifiably hoped they would be saved.

Or another: How someone ill with an incurable disease decided he wouldn't go see the appropriate doctors, but would treat himself instead; however, to everyone's surprise, he died soon after.

Also: This one person, trusting his inner voice, which is supposed to help us find a way out of just about any situation, went into the mountains and, against everyone's expectations, never came back.

Or this one: How, against all reasonable expectations, a man who'd lost his legs died before receiving the prostheses, with which he was meant to have learned to dance—everyone was unpleasantly surprised by that one.

Or the person caught in the thick of battle who, rather unexpectedly, dies in the most ordinary way, rather than coming back safe and sound, as it ought to be, normally.

And here's a totally unbelievable one: A person has a noose put around his neck, the stool is knocked out from under him and he hangs there dead as a doornail in the noose, rather than anything else that one might naturally expect from him.

And here's another one: A fire is built under someone, the flames are flaring up around him, everyone—nervously, but with great curiousity—watches to see how he will manage to avoid a tragic outcome, but instead he, screaming and wailing, fails to escape, much to the surprise of those gathered around.

Or, for example: A man is grabbed by his hair, thrust into water, held there without breathing for 20–25 minutes, and is then let go, and though all confidently expect him to emerge alive from the water, he slowly surfaces as a heavy and unwieldy corpse, which comes as a profound and unpleasant surprise to everyone.

BRAIN POWER

(1998)

Advisory Note

It goes without saying that brain power determines little in our business. In this, our most delicate business—the art of generating the artistic. However, thus far, this is—alas!—the only thing that can be more or less precisely defined and expressed in the proper form.

It is well known that Tolstoy was 2.5 times smarter than Chekhov.

Dostoevsky, meanwhile, depending on the season and cyclical fluctuations, was either 3 times smarter than Tolstoy or twice as stupid.

Chekhov, for his part, was 24 times smarter than Potapenko.

It follows that Tolstoy was 60 times smarter than Potapenko.

Dostoevsky, meanwhile, depending on the previously described conditions, was either 7.5 times smarter than Chekhov, or 1.25 times.

And as for Potapenko—Dostoevsky was either 180 times smarter than him or only 30 times.

We will pass over the details relating to Kuprin, Bunin, Remizov, Zamyatin, Bulgakov, Sholokhov, Vaginov, and Dobychin.

We end up with the following distribution:

For Tolstoy—70, 7, 40, 30, 28, 25, 4, 6.

For Dostoevsky—210 and 35, 120 and 20, 90 and 15, 84 and 14, 75 and 12, 5, 12 and 2, 18 and 3.

For Chekhov—28, 2.8, 16, 12, 11.2, 10, 1.6, 2.4.

And now, let us talk about something completely different.

The data suggests that Platonov was Sorokin's equal in brain power; in any event, this can be assumed.

However, in a different system than the one to which Tolstoy, Dostoevsky, Chekhov, et al., belong, which we may label as A.

Then, in the system of Platonov, Sorokin would be labeled B.

Under these circumstances the brain power of Tolstoy in relation to Platonov, Sorokin would be A:B.

In relation to Dostoevsky in the variants 3A:B and 0.5A:B.

And in relation to Chekhov: 0.4A:B.

The coefficients in relation to the remaining objects of system A can be determined in a similar fashion.

And when we postulate or define further systems (B, C, D, U, F, and so on), the same model may be used to calculate the brain power of whomever you like.

NON-SPURIOUS

TRANSFORMATIONS

(1998)

Advisory Note

The continuous processes of transformation of everything into everything, all of these cosmic and simpler everyday combinatorics, exist because of the limited amount of existing material for all and any processes (given, of course, this—quite lengthy, in human terms—process), and infinite existence, and the space appropriate for this existence, at least in logical terms.

And in this infinity we tend to highlight, according to our preference, either the real axiology or the version of it that we read into the general process of *nirgunam*, being without distinctions. And why wouldn't we? Especially since our axiology isn't so hot. Just a simple logical progression, or really just our desire for it. Including our, as it were, logically progressive sole and single act, a teeny-tiny act, in some other grandiose and—because of its grandiosity—possibly (so thought our hero) life-saving logical progression. That is, if you follow the progression, you'll be saved. Oh, but you can't remember everything, you can't follow through on everything. Yet, we hope, the very principle of universal transformability will be sufficiently and completely reflected in our small example.

That's it.

If you take two tables and put them together, and put a chair on top of them, you get a throne.

If you take the throne, flip the tables onto one side, and put a chair behind them, you get a machine gun nest.

If you take the machine-gun nest, put one table on top of the other, and throw out the chair, you get a pagoda.

If you take the pagoda, turn one of the tables upside down and submerge it in water, and throw out the other table, you get a flotation device.

If you take the flotation device, remove the table from the water, stand it up normally, put the other table on top of it, hoist a bookcase up on top of them, and attach a lamp on top, you get a lighthouse.

If you take the lighthouse, throw out the two tables and the bookcase, take a bureau, and put wheels under it, you get an armored car.

If you take the armored car, get rid of the wheels, pull out the bureau drawers, stand them up vertically, and get rid of the bureau, you get a columbarium.

If you take the columbarium, throw away the bureau drawers, take the chair and lay it on its back, put a stool behind it and turn on the fan, you get an airplane.

If you take the airplane, stand the chair up normally, put another one on top, then a third, then a fourth, and as many as the height of the room allows, you will get a descent into the mine.

If you take the descent into the mine and topple it to the floor with a crash so that you end up with a pile of debris, you get the Spanish Armada after the Battle of Trafalgar.

If you take the Spanish Armada, throw away the debris, stand up one of the surviving chairs normally, and connect it to electricity, you get an electric chair.

If you take the electric chair, throw away the actual chair and let a large jolt of electricity run through the disconnected wires, having attached capacitors to them, you get lightning.

If you take the lightning, take a person and touch them to one of the wires, you get a corpse.

If you take the corpse, throw everything else away, bring in a bed, and put two opposite- or same-sex beings in it, you get love.

If you take love, get rid of the bed, attach wings to the backs of the two beings, you get angels.

If you take the angels, get rid of the beings, and substantially whittle down the wings, you get Spirit.

If you take the Spirit, get rid of everything, and bring nothing in, then, in fact, nothing will be left, but whether there will be Nothing—that is the question.

RECALCULATING TIME

(1997)

Advisory Note

Everything that happens, happens, if you'll excuse me, in real time. The issue is not of time, but of reality. And this is exactly what we want to figure out, using what appear to be the concepts and terminology of the units of measurement of time.

Numerous generations of young people all over the world

Thrown into the jaws of war and similar feathered chimeras

Go, turning their young smiling faces

From old chronicles and documentary films

During the last century, along with collateral victims of wars, about 350 million of them were killed

At the age of about 20 years, having missed 50 of the years allotted to them on average

In total, all together, they missed 350 million times 50 years = 16.5 billion years

With the current population of the Earth calculated at 4 billion

And in real time, for the entire century, we tentatively take the number 6.5 billion

Subtracting the dead we get: 6.5 billion - 350 million = 6.15 billion

And also subtracting about one third of the ones who did not live to 20 years: 6,150 ÷ 3 = 2.05 billion

Now we divide 16.5 by 2.05, and we get

As much as 8 additional years for each person

From which, naturally, the ones capable of bearing the weight of these abstractly indicated virtual years constitute no more than 5%

Thus each capable one gets assigned 160 excess years

I recall how mindlessly I wasted time as a young man

Throwing it away on entertainment, boozing and other nonsense

And only later did I realize the tragedy and irreplaceability of this

Assuming that a normal day's work requires 10 hours in order to achieve some visible results

That is, based on the beginning of meaningful existence from 15 years of age in 1953 up to 35 years of age in 1975

I worked, by the calculated average no more than 20% of the time, that is, 365 days times 20 = 7300 days, which, multiplied by 10 hours, equals 73,000 hours

I worked a total of 12,600 hours and wasted 60,400

I would not count the period from 1975 to 1985, since I worked during it according to the above-indicated proper norm

From 1986 to 1996 I came to my senses and added 10% in intensity

By reducing the shortfall to 3650 working hours, there was still a shortfall of 56,250 hours

If in the next few years I am able to increase the intensity of my work by 30%

At that intensity I'd have to work for 56 years

In order to reach a net of zero

So, if you add my current 56 to these 56

It turns out that I ought to hold on for 112 years, until 2052

While this would be a highly unusual case, nevertheless, it is not impossible

They say that a year in prison goes by like two

But considering the tremendous stresses of life today, if a year doesn't go by like two, it's still something like one and half

Well, I suppose I didn't feel this in childhood

But starting around age 18

So from my current 56 we can subtract 18 and get 38, and multiply that by one and half, we get 75, then add back in the unsullied 18

Also, my current life as a professional artist is no gift

It's an anxious and crazy existence, with maybe a coefficient of 1.8

I started it at about age 35

Therefore, my age is already $(75 - 35) \times 1.8 + 35 = 107$ years

Moreover, considering the hostility that my specific extraordinary personality has provoked throughout my entire life, we may add in a psychological complexity coefficient of 0.3, and so we get: $107 + 31.1 = 139.1$

Well, add in this and that and another 10 to 12 years gets tacked on easy

So my present age can be estimated at 141 years

If you take Pushkin's tragic 37

Given the current shifted norms

Which include a late maturation, relative to the times

The first 10 years, from the age of 15 to their maturation, to the present 25

We have a coefficient of 1.8 increase such that $37 - 10 + 18 = 45$

Well, of course, our accelerated pace of life, which temporarily capsizes at the time of entrance into economic activity from about 27 years, would have meant for him, Pushkin, a reduction factor of 1.3 $(45 - 26) \div 1.3 + 26 = 15 + 26 = 41$

However, his intelligence and the effect on his maturation of his quiet and thoughtful life, naturally and unequivocally indicate a coefficient of 3

And if you take those years to be at least a third of his life, we get $41 \div 3 \times 3 + 41 - 41 \div 3 = 41 + 14 = 55$ years

Well, then you tack on another 6 to 7 years, and the result is 62 years—not bad

And if you take all these factors into their opposite value: $-1.8 + 173 - 3 = -3.5$

And if you compare this with the years of my maturity, my age would be $(56 - 25) \div 3 + 25 = $ I'd only be 35

They say that in the entire history of humanity no more than 10 billion persons have lived on earth

This is not me saying this, this is science talking

And if you take an average life expectancy, based on the extremely short lives people had before—30 years

Then we get 30 billion people-years

And accordingly, 10.095 trillion people-days

And accordingly, 65.7 trillion people-hours

And accordingly, 394.2 trillion people-minutes

Now, if we take the average weight of a person over all of that time, given that ancient people weighed very, very little—50 kg

And if we imagine this proto-human, who bore the whole burden of life

Then we get a load of 39.4 billion minutes per 1 kilogram of live weight

And, accordingly, 39.42 billion years to 1 gram of live weight

And if you imagine the life expectancy of life on Earth at 4000 years

We get 1,013 thousand years per 1 gram of live weight per year

And we get 278 years at 1 gram per day

And, at 23 years for one gram of live weight in one hour

And 0.8 years to 1 gram per minute

And finally, 0.013 years for one gram per second

VERDICTS

(1998)

Advisory Note

Since the Middle Ages animals have been put on trial for violating the su-
preme, metaphorical, social, and human order (themselves, incidentally,
understood and consciously laid out, if not as a pure reproduction of meta-
physical order, then as its purest possible reflection). They recognized the
conscious (what, you think dogs are stupid? they're smarter than some of us)
or half-conscious (given each and every animal species belonging to a em-
powered communal soul) assumption of responsibility for the representation
of, at the very least, the forces of light or darkness.

As a reflection of the fundamental world-organizing foundations of not only
human, but all of existence, these judicial proceedings, were and, at times,
served as the only guarantee of a person's belonging not only to his earthly
but also his world-building, world-founding energy and activity. Sometimes
these were the only defense against the invasion of the destructive forces of
entropy.

The Bear, for negligent performance of duty, shall be sentenced to two years probation with deduction of 50% of salary at his place of permanent employment; who objects to what? No one and to nothing.

The Hare, for petty theft, shall be sentenced to administrative discipline at his place of permanent residence; who objects to what? No one and to nothing.

The Dog, for hooliganism, shall be sentenced to one year of imprisonment, but having been given a good reference from his place of work, this shall be changed to 15 days and public service, get it! You don't get it? You get it, alright!

The Cat, for the systematic violation of public order and antisocial behavior, shall be sentenced to exile at a distance of 100 kilometers—and no objections! What do you have to object to?

The Wolf, for large-scale embezzlement, shall be sentenced to 25 years, or no, to be shot would be better, no, it's still more fair to say 25 years with confiscation of property—you think that's harsh? No, not really! It can't be done any other way.

The Rat, for antisocial behavior and insulting accepted norms and the political system, shall be sentenced to 5 years of hard labor, followed by a 10-year suspension of civil rights! Too little? But our judicial system is not punitive! It is humanist and instructional! We aren't Fascists, after all.

The Wild Boar, for a disagreeable appearance, shall be sentenced to death by being eaten—and rightly so! Though what good will it do! What, like you do things differently?!

The Bird, for treason, shall be sentenced to death and the confiscation of property, to teach others to not do it.

The Echidna, for an anti-human appearance and overall nastiness, shall be sentenced to be shot with subsequent rehabilitation, so that there will be some order, after all, and high justice will triumph.

The Elephant, for its huge size, which is an assault on human honor and dignity, shall be crossed off the list of existing beings, and its ongoing existence shall be considered an anomaly and a phantom.

For economic, moral, political and behavioral crimes the polecat, fox, squirrel, badger, chipmunk, vole, jay, lark, raven and crow, deer and badger, kangaroo and its joeys, whale and shark, pike, swan and crab, and all their ilk, shall be sentenced to various terms of punishment in various places, but with a strictly legal and individual approach to each specific case, that no indiscriminate leveling and wholesale depersonalization take place.

The Cockroach shall simply be sentenced to be shot; this needs no explanation.

The Lion shall be sentenced to public humiliation and degradation, since it is clear that the king of animals, nature, and everything else is man.

Rivers shall be sentenced to be redirected in all possible directions, as a result of which they shall run shallow and dry up—which is only fair.

The Sun shall be sentenced to exposure and public repentance, with consequent removal from the lists of remembrance and glorification of anything beginning with the words: Long live! So it must be.

Decisions for all the remaining cases are being prepared, and the sentences will be announced as they are decided within a reasonable period of time. None will be exempt.

LETTERS

(1997)

Advisory Note

We have already had one occasion to describe something like this. But the articulated development, the composition, as it were, the cultivation of the graceful plant of meaning from letters as ontological units, presented like a picture composed of historically determined acts scattered across different times and peoples lined up in their quasi-processual manner—how can such a thing not bewitch the seeking, subtly-feeling soul and not compel it to renew its search for similar, deeply moving proto-events.

To pronounce the first letter he drives off God knows where, changing trains and then stagecoaches, wrapped up in a heavy gray cape against the rain and wind, flinging open the oaken doors of some tavern or other, holing up in a corner, and, glancing periodically over his shoulder out a small, dark and dirty window, says **E**, and finds himself on the Polish-Lithuanian border.

To pronounce the second letter he finds it most convenient to turn into a shock-worker of the second five-year plan, or something like that, and, at the dizzying height of the blast furnace under construction, loudly, almost defiantly, exhales into the sparkling air: **V**.

To pronounce the third letter he finds himself a little child clad in a white and blue sailor suit, roaming around an old-fashioned garden, wandering into an unfamiliar gazebo, in deep silence tracing a pale, thin little finger on the dusty marble parapet the outline of an unexpectedly emerging **A**.

Then he finds himself in delirium, either following difficult and failed childbirth, or brought by strange peasants from the nearby battlefield to a dark hut where he lay, surrounded by a mountain of the enemies he'd destroyed, or after having been tossed about by the fates or agents of the secret police, in a fever, shouts: **N-nnn**!

To pronounce the next letter he runs in the form of a beast with long ears hanging down, a curly tail, blue eyes surrounded by long, silky, dark lashes, turns around in response to someone's muffled stirring in the darkness of the bushes and says, stammering slightly: **G-gggg**!

Further still he is forced to crawl in the form of some kind of insect over numerous obstacles, not daring to even raise his head, just persistently and inexorably dragging some tremendous weight, howling: **E-eee!**

To pronounce the seventh letter he simply becomes some sort of little cell, struggling in the blood flow to reach the shuddering, brilliant heart, penetrating into it and loudly exploding into bits even smaller than its tiny self, and exclaiming: **L-lll!**

To pronounce the penultimate letter he stands in the middle of the clearing as a huge oak tree, creaking and swaying, and to the prince driving past it, to the peasant walking past, to the city-dweller, the fugitive, the thief, the murderer, to a child, to a bird flying past, to a beast, a madman, a hero, a chieftain, an insect, a stranger, to the *genius loci*, a mermaid, a snake and a hedgehog, to local Tahitian and Chinese women, to philosopher and anthroposophist, carpenter and painter, to an actor, to a miner, to an infant and an owner, to the kleptomaniac and the drug addict, to the cat and the dog, to the Roman and the Jew, alike, he says: **I.**

To pronounce the last letters, **ON**, an extraordinary thunderstorm breaks out, rumbling and flashing, with wild energy, but quickly calms down and is replaced by a picture of unimaginable peace, glistening with wet grass and leaves under the rays of the emergent sun.

And now, to gather all of this together he holes up in the furthest secluded room, shuts the door, not even letting in the cat he loves to the point of weakness, bends over the table, takes up tweezers and a scalpel and then some other devices, then discards them, and with only the strength of his sprawling, searing mind and his powerful and purposeful will, through his hot heart's irresistible beating, he collects it all into a word that hangs in the air, luminous in the middle of all this, the word EVANGELION, the Gospel.

RUSSIA AND DEATH

(1997)

Advisory Note

This really shouldn't be taken to be some kind of mysticism. These are just simple snapshots of everyday life, espied by an interested and attentive gaze. Well, perhaps it has all gotten a little dried out by the fires of utópia and the passions of an apocalyptically-minded intelligentsia. But nevertheless has been seen from a seventh-floor window of a ten-story building in Belyaevo. All this came into being in the snow-sprinkled spaces, by one running away from my foyer towards unknown, western distances disappearing beyond the horizon, in the direction of the setting sun, which, however, it being winter, didn't even bother rising in the first place.

Here are the snapshots.

§

Once Russia came to Death and asked: How will we live?

Times five, answers Death

But five? That's a complicated number. If, for example, you subtract 2 from five, you get 3

§

Once again Russia came to Death and asked again: How will we live?

Death looked at Russia. Evidently, she didn't understand her.

In positive 4, she answers.

But this positive 4 is a number that's not quite a number, even. If you take one away and add positive 9, you get almost 13. Or really 12 with two pluses, which have nowhere to go

§

Then Death came to Russia and said: How can this be?

Russia looked at her, caught her drift, and said: In what sense do you want to know?

In the sense of the value of zero!

But a zero is a number that is almost non-existent. Or rather, super-existent. That is, if you add something to it, or subtract, then it deceptively makes an appearance. But if you add a zero, then everything is as it should be

§

But then Death came to Russia in the guise of Russia and asked: Well, so, how now?

But Russia cannot answer herself, even in the reasonable guise of Death, and cannot answer the reverse, but only confirms the evaluation

But, then, if you take the number -1, it can be added to anything at all, while remaining itself all the while

§

So then Russia came to Death in the form of Death and asked: So, will we live?

And Death recognized Russia as pure, unadulterated duplicity, and answered:

To you I reply as honestly as to my own self: 7!

But the number 7 equals 63, when translated according to the order
of the letters in the Russian alphabet: C (19) + E (6) + M (14) +
b (24) = 63

§

But then they come separately to each other, that is, Russia to
Russia, and Death to Death, but ask and answer one and the same
thing: 25!

And what does 25 mean? Well, if you divide by 5, then you get
5—nothing special. If you take away 2, then you get 23—and that
is rather more extraordinary. If you take away 10, then you get 15.
If you take away 16, then all you have left is 9. If you add 7, you get
32. But if you add 10 and subtract 35, then you get the long-
awaited 0

§

But in the end they came to me and asked: Will we live?

We will, we will, my dear sweet girls!

It's a simple number: the two of them, plus me—and there you
have three. And if you add everything else—you get four. Oh, plus
God—then you get five

THREE SOURCES

SOURCES

(1998)

Advisory Note

Since the time of Lenin and Leninism it has been known that everything has three sources. Well, we are not as shrewd and powerful in our capacity to trace them with striking precision. But we did try. Moreover, our errors cannot lead to such dangerous and devastating consequences as in Lenin's case. Ours are just little jokes, slips of the tongue, grimaces.

There are three sources of knowledge: life, books, plus something unexpected. For instance, an ex-convict who moved into the neighborhood.

There are three sources of life: food, love, plus something unexpected. For instance, maybe there is some kind of God.

There are three sources of love: the heart, the libido, plus something unexpected. A mental injury, for example, that fundamentally changes one's perspective on life.

There are three sources of anger: bad temper, liver trouble, plus something unexpected. An evil spirit, for instance, that has possessed the organism.

There are three sources of weakness: ill health, a bad climate, plus something unexpected. For instance, a streetcar falling suddenly into one's path, or something heavy.

There are three sources of well-being: hard work, resourcefulness, plus something unexpected. For instance, the death of a rich relative, having good credit, or finding a purse stuffed with dollars. Which, of course, in this era of credit cards and electronic money, is a highly improbable illusion.

There are three sources of death: predestined inadequacies of the body, passionate desires and the penalty for them, well, and something unexpected, too. For instance, a face-to-face encounter with a Basilisk or the Medusa.

ON EMPTINESS

(1999)

Advisory Note

There are no direct, unambiguously correct answers to the question of emptiness. The only answers are evasive and skittering. But the method and direction of the skittering, like the space that curves around a black hole, is precisely what allows us to reason about emptiness more or less definitively.

Is emptiness male or female? Or...?

This question is answered: Yes

Does emptiness begin with anything, or does anything end in emptiness?

This question is answered: Yes

Or it is answered: Maybe

Or a third answer: Everything will work out

Does emptiness have an appearance or use?

This question is answered very simply

Is emptiness one or two?

This question is answered to whatever extent necessary

Does emptiness think of itself in terms of emptiness or fullness?

This question should not always be answered

Is emptiness generated by itself or by something else, which can also generate something else?

This question should be answered evasively

Does emptiness manifest in something else or only in emptiness?

This question is answered by giving two thumbs up

Is emptiness visible, palpable, or only graspable speculatively?

This question is answered by joining two fingers in a circle

Is it worth doing a favor for emptiness or borrowing anything from it?

This question is answered with a nod of the head

Are you silent because you are emptiness or because you have nothing to say about emptiness?

This question is answered with charged silence

Is everything in emptiness for the sake of emptiness or is there something that exceeds it?

This question is answered through absence

Can emptiness reveal only emptiness, or is it that through emptiness all is manifested, and does all that manifests through emptiness reveals emptiness, or its total redundancy?

This question should be answered through emptiness

THE BATHERS

(1996)

Advisory Note

Once, I was swimming in a river and thought to myself (and what doesn't one think of!): So, who is next to me now, and indeed, over the years, the centuries (not millennia, of course—this water is not primordial, not the Water of Life), who else has gone in, come out of, and bathed in it, in this water? It could really be anyone at all. The price of universal commonality is indeterminacy and a lack of commitment, and, in a sense, a kind of non-existence (in the narrow, earthly sense). But in private, upper-echelon (including even the heavenly upper echelons) bodies of water—well, not necessarily of water, bodies of whatever—the users can be, if not counted on one hand, then at least identified with certain circles. In certain milieu the bathers can be identified by a kind of exceptional sense of belonging, involvement, or affinity.

And defining the affinity of this milieu and its bathers constitutes a special, specific little buzz for us, which does not obligate anyone else whatsoever to come to any conclusions or decisions.

I would like to note that the aforementioned milieu and the categories to which their bathers can be associated does not at all exhaust the plenitude of such relations in the world, but we nevertheless believe that the critical mass of these examples and studies is sufficient to serve as a methodological (or even ideological) basis for this perception of the structurally complex and intricately interconnected world, as well as for further research and appropriations should anyone desire to undertake such.

Who bathes in gold?

Those who bathe in gold are the rich, Americans, Tsars, Arabs, Jews, misers, gold-miners, visionaries, and villains

Those who bathe in gold

Are simply called

The gold-bathers

Who bathes in silver?

Those who bathe in silver are the desert-dwellers, the people of the moonlight, thieves, mystics, Tibetans, night owls like myself, cats, chamois deer, Cappadocians, and those born internally

He who bathes in silver

Is often called

The Seer of reflected light

Who bathes in water?

Those who bathe in water are fish, sailors, virgins, smooth-skinned neurotics, Greeks, rats, killers, children with Down syndrome, mermaids, all manner of no-see-ums, and certain government figures

He who bathes in water

Is called, simply

A bather

Who is bathed in the glow?

Those who bathe in the glow are the heroes basking in the glow of glory, bastards in the glow of greed, children in beams of love, brides in the glow of conquest and submission, misanthropes with their heavy glowering, and in the glow of their common experience—firemen, locksmiths, milkmen, doormen, nurses, and students

He who is bathed in the glow

Is inevitably called

The one who surrenders his body to the flow

Next, naturally, comes the question:

And who is bathed in shit?

Almost everyone bathes in shit

But especially sewage-pipe cleaners, teachers, artists, proctologists, fibbers, honest politicians, compassionate women, and cavalrymen

He who bathes in shit

Naturally, is called…

Well, he's called various things

Who bathes or wallows in himself?

Those who bathe or wallow in themselves are the sick, the healthy, the half-sick, the ratted-on, the defeated, Russians and people who like Russian literature, Nietzsche, Dostoevsky, schoolgirls, girls from the factory school, hesychasts, and the man who tried to remove his own appendix

He who wallows in himself

Is called

A self-wallower

Who doesn't wallow in anything at all?

Those who don't wallow in anything are weightlifters, cooks, ancient Germans, monks, merchants of the Second Guild, the homeless, football players, Chapayevites, and contemporaries of Simeon of Polotsk

Those who don't wallow in anything

Are in fact not called

Anything

Who is awash in nothing?

Those who bathe in the nothing are negative theologians, Indians, alcoholics, certain mathematicians, absolute aphasics, babies, meteorologists, chess players, and demolition experts

He who bathes in nothing

Is wildly named

Absolved

Who is awash in everything?

Those bathed in the all are everyone, but not in their individuality, rather gathered together into enormous hyper-communal bodies

Those overlapping communal religious and natural bodies, themselves bathing in the force fields they themselves generate

WHO I WANTED TO KILL
AT VARIOUS AGES

(1997)

Advisory Note

This text is among several of my preceding ones that have as their objective to denominate—in a nearly catalog-like and enumerative fashion—names, events, thoughts (instantaneous and lingering), intentions, projects, and desires with reference to certain either concrete or invented/mythologized circumstances. And, generally speaking, all these explanations are unimportant. What's important is the energy of the flow of real and imagined positions of remembrance and usage.

Compared to the others, this text may seem to be, as it were, the most bloodthirsty. Come on, really! First of all, it isn't any more bloodthirsty than the other bloodthirsty texts. Secondly, who can correctly and accurately catalogue the phantoms of childhood and youth?! So don't bother trying to think all this through. Relax and observe the flow, aligned and channeled more or less correctly and efficiently.

As a child I wanted to kill Hitler

Really it wasn't just me, everyone wanted to

I also wanted to kill Antonescu

That's just how I was

And I also wanted to kill the evil old lady in the neighboring apartment

And I wanted to kill her cat, to make her cry

And I wanted to kill the neighbor, but just for fun

And I wanted to kill Syngman Rhee

Though no, no, I had only wanted to kill him later

And there were many, many, many others that I wanted to kill, who had themselves already died

As a teenager, I wanted kill Truman, Adenauer, and Tito

And I wanted to kill this one redneck in our courtyard, nicknamed Toad

I also wanted to kill our school principal because he was mean

And because he was mean, I also wanted to kill the chemistry teacher

And later I wanted to kill my lady chemistry teacher

And I also wanted to kill Genghis Khan, Batu, Napoleon, and the dastardly Teutonic knights that tortured Russia

Also, I wanted to kill Vitalik Borisov, but only as a joke, to teach him a lesson, but I did want to kill him

I wanted to kill Bukharin, Trotsky, Kamenev, Zinoviev, Rykov, Tukhachevsky, Slansky, Krylenko, Radek, the doctors, the military men, the technicians, the writers, the Jews, the Georgians, the Germans, the Americans, the Japanese, and many, many, many others, who had already died, but I still wanted to kill them

In my youth I wanted to kill Stalin, Kaganovich, Malenkov, Molotov, Zhdanov, Yezhov, Beria, Poskrebyshev, Dzerzhinsky, Menzhinsky, and, uh, that guy, I've forgotten his name, but I wanted to kill him, too

And also in my youth I wanted to kill that lady, what's her name, no, no, I didn't want to kill her, I wanted to kill her much later—what's her name again?

And also, I wanted to kill, in my youth, Vasyuta the gangster from the next block, and it's too bad that I didn't kill him

And I wanted to kill the kid we called The Seal from our block

And also, from our block, I wanted to kill The Rat, in my youth

And Tolya, in my youth I wanted to kill him, too, though he was from another block

And I also wanted to kill Batista, Samoza, Mao Zedong, Lin Biao, Tshombe, Mobutu, Semichastny, Pavlov, and many, many, many others, whom I don't even remember anymore, who had already died on their own before the time in my youth when I wanted to kill them

In later years I wanted to kill Vuchetich, although no, no, I didn't want to kill him

I wanted to kill Serov, but no, no, I didn't want to kill him

I wanted to kill Surov, but no, no, no, I didn't want to, I did not want to kill him

I wanted to kill Brezhnev too, although no, no, no, no, no, no, I didn't want to

I wanted to kill Brodsky, but no, I didn't want to

Others wanted to kill him, but I didn't want to, I didn't want to, I didn't want to

And I didn't want to kill Rubenstein

And I didn't want to kill Nekrasov

And I didn't want to kill Sorokin

But that guy—what's his name?—I wanted to kill him

Yet, overall, I didn't want to kill anybody, no one, no one, except for certain people

Other people certainly wanted to kill me, but I didn't want to, didn't want to, didn't want to, didn't want to, didn't want to kill anybody

Yet, in principle, who can you kill?

Well, you can kill practically anybody

Like you can kill this guy? Sure you can

Can you kill Yeltsin? Yeah, sure you can

Can you kill Anpilov? You can

But what, you're not allowed to kill Erofeyev? I wouldn't really want to, but it's possible

So what, you're not allowed to kill the youth? It's totally doable

But your son, your son, your son, you can't kill your son! Why ever not? You can

And your wife, your wife, your wife, you can't kill her? Why ever not? Because you can't! you can't! you can't! You can, you can

And I can't kill you, right? Why ever not? You can indeed

I thought about how it's probably not allowed to kill the Patriarch. Why not, if they killed God, why not kill the Patriarch? It's possible

A LIST OF MY OWN DEATHS

OWN DEATHS

(1999)

Advisory Note

I myself was surprised to discover, after the fact, that three of my recent major "inventory" texts are associated with the theme of mortality—those who died in my time, the enumeration of graves, and this one here, too. I thought that I might just as well have listed, to no lesser effect, things that were lively and cheerful. But then it occurred to me that the principle of inventory itself is mortification *par excellence*. So, quite naturally, the most natural thematic addition to this would be something correspondingly mortal. It's simply a case of like being drawn to like.

I might have died at age 1 from chickenpox, but didn't

At 2, I might have died from measles

At 3, I might have died from lupus, hunger, and war

In my 4th year, I could have died from measles, many did

Oh, and at 6 months I could have died from dyspepsia

I also might have died before my birth, from the unspeakable difficulties of the life to come

I could have died while being born, these things happen

I could have died at 5 from scarlet fever—a terrible thing

At 6, 7, 8, and 9, I could have died from polio

At 10, I could have died from fear—it was very scary

At 11 and 12, I could have died of boredom at school, but I prevailed

At 13 and 14, I could have died while crossing the street, in someone else's garden stealing apples, or in one of those brutal alley fights

At 15, I could have died of encephalitis from a tick bite in a forest outside Moscow

At 16, I could have just died

I could have just died at 17

I could have just died at 18

I could have died at 19 or 20 when bathing in the Black or Baltic Seas

At 24, I could have died from the police

At 25 years of age, I could have died from food poisoning

I could have died at the ages of 27, 28, 29, 30, 31, 32, 33, 34, 35, 36, 37, 38, 39, 40, or 41, in prisons, camps, from torture, on a prisoners' bunk, during interrogations, in the logging camps, by a criminal's knife, at the North Pole, eaten up by gnats, in the desert, on a cross, thrust under the ice, thrown into the furnace, on the rack, from a bullet, in a dungeon, in manacles, from exhaustion in the cattle wagon, in a gas chamber, thrown from a cliff, doused in acid, from scurvy, without making it to the location of my second prison term, or from a heart attack in front of the camp gates as they were flung open in the days of rehabilitation

At 41, I could have also died from a twisted intestine

Or, at 40, for example, if I hadn't died before that in prison, I could have died from being bitten by a rabid dog—they were running around Moscow in those days

And at 39, I might have died from malaria in Asia

But at age 42, I could have already died of tuberculosis

I could have died at 43 from a traumatic head injury, for example, from a blow with an ax

I could have died at 44, 45 and 46 from something or other, literally just some nonsense

I could have died at 47 from serious worries

I could have died at 48 from a possible cancer

At 49, 50, 51, I could have died from a heart attack, and indeed I did die, but I snapped out of it

At 52, I could still die from a heart attack

At 53, I could die from anything, for example, from an incorrect way of life

I could have died at 54 from just about anything

I could have died at 55 from anything

I could have died at 56 from anything

I could have died at 57 from anything

I could have died at 58 from anything

And at my present 59 years, I could die from anything, for example from these compositions

And in all the years, times, and sentences to come, I can, can, can die, die, die—from what, from what, from what?—from just about anything

LIST OF OBSERVATIONS

(1998)

Advisory Note

A list of the buried, departed, those who've laid down their heads on the battlefield and in domestic squabbles, those called for help or as witnesses—this is no novelty in literary, quasi-literary, and para-literary practice. The current list is simply the result of regular observations of burial sites in a cemetery in Russia; the very regularity of these burial sites, as well as their almost statistically disinterested listing, calms and pacifies while at the same time assigning administratively a title and rank to death, if not to its results. So, in fact, the incidental results of any kind of activity are practically impossible to grasp or predict. And, in any case, their incidentality makes them inessential.

What I see:

Glebov, Ivan F., b. March 1792

Died—January 1828

Glebova, Maria Platonovna, b. August 1788

Died in August—August 1875

Glebov, Makar Ivanovich, b. Dec. 1815

Died—September 1875

Glebov, Fedor Ivanovich, b. September 1819

Died—January 1823—a mere babe in arms!

Glebova, Pauline Ivanovna, b. May 1825

Died—February 1867—evidently died an old maid

Grigoriev, Kozma Apollonovich, b. July 1865

Died—April 1897—that sounds really, really familiar! But no, I can't recall.

I keep looking:

Ivan Ivanovich Pappiniano—must be an Italian—died in 1957, and born—1898

Grigorieva, Lenina Pavlovna, December 1924-September 1978

Gustavov, Yan Gerbertovich—maybe a German, maybe Polish 1875-1928

Gustavova, Irina Kazimirovna—unclear who she was, but anyway, she lived! from 1880 to 1961.

OK

I keep looking:

Dudalin, Paul Antonovich—1899-1971

Dudalina, Evegenia Semenovna—1901-1962—wow, that's rare, she didn't outlive her husband

Dudalin, Peter Pavlovich—1920-1941—wow, the father outlived the son by so many years

Dudalin, Gregory Pavlovich—1922-1947—damn, and he outlived his second son

Dudalina, Maria P.—1925-1940—wow, outlived his daughter too

But he didn't outlive his other kids

Didn't outlive two daughters

And here's another son he didn't outlive

They must have all been pretty healthy

Dudalin, Athanasius Grigorovich—1893-1937—a relative, or just someone with the same last name, maybe they were friends, drank together, fought... who knows

OK

I keep looking:

Ordinin, Ignatius Provovich—1812-1837—wowee, look when he
saw fit to get born! And then he died along with Pushkin.

Sharapov, Ravil Akhmetovich—must be a Tatar—1937-1991

Kushnareva, Dina Isaakovna—and she's Jewish—1937-1988

I keep looking:

Surname worn away, Ivan Nikolayevich—1911-1958

Keep looking:

Surname worn away, name worn away, patronymic—Nikolaevich—
1917—second date worn away

Surname worn away, Ivan, patronymic worn away—1780-1820

Surname worn away, name worn away, patronymic worn away—
1775-1831

Keep looking:

Surname worn away, name worn away, patronymic worn away, first
date worn away, second date—1877

Keep looking:

Surname worn away, name worn away, patronymic worn away, dates
worn away

Surname worn away, name worn away, patronymic worn away, dates
worn away

Surname worn away, name worn away, patronymic worn away—
1921-1958

I keep looking:

Surname worn away, name worn away, patronymic worn away, dates worn away

Surname worn away, name worn away, patronymic worn away, dates worn away

Keep looking:

Last name, first name, dates—worn away

Last name, first name, dates—worn away

Last name, first name, dates—worn away

Keep looking

All worn away

Keep looking

Keep looking

All worn away

All worn away

All worn away

Keep looking

All worn away

All worn away

All worn away

All worn away

All worn away

All worn away

Keep looking

Worn away

Worn away

Farther

Farther

Worn away

ЗДРАВСТВОВАТЬ ВСЕМ!

М. МИРРАХИМОВ,

член-корреспондент АН СССР, лауреат Государственной премии СССР, Киргизская ССР

В СОЛНЕЧНЫЙ день самолёт может уже через два часа вас доставить на дрейфующую станцию.

ОТМЕЧЕН УСПЕХ

Ю. АЛЕКСАНДРОВ,
Вологодская область.

С ДОБРЫМ СЛОВОМ

А. АРТЮНЯН

Как одна бригада

Е. КЛИНЧЕНКО

В А Х Т РАБОТАЕТ

ПРОРЫВАЯСЬ

Факт и коммента́рии

ПАРТИЙНАЯ ЖИЗНЬ: НА ОБЛАСТНЫХ КОНФЕРЕНЦИЯХ

М. ПОЛТОРАНИН

В. ЛИСИН

(Соб. корр. «Правды»)

г. Тюмень.

COMMENTARIES

SOURCES FOR THE TEXTS

For the translations in this edition, where possible, I chose to use texts from collections published in the Prigov's lifetime, which the author would have most likely checked and approved. These were also the books that I happened to collect while I was becoming acquainted with the author's work.

This edition also relies for certain clarifications, and for one whole piece, on the recent editions of collected works in five-volumes edited by Mark Lipovetsky and published by NLO (Novoe Literaturnoe Obozrenie) in Moscow.

The sources of the texts are listed below, with abbreviations that will be used in the commentaries, in case they may be useful to readers interested in the originals, and in the particular publications of the texts (which may vary from collection to collection) that these translations follow.

ST: *Soviet Texts, 1979–1984*. Saint Petersburg, 1997. Ivan Limbach. (Советские тексты, 1979–1984. Санкт-Петербург, 1997. Издательство Ивана Лимбаха.)

EPS: *EPS*: Viktor Erofeyev, Dmitri Prigov, Vladimir Sorokin. Moscow, 2002. zebraE. (ЕПС: Виктор Ерофеев, Дмитрий Пригов, Владимир Сорокин. Москва, 2002. зебраЕ.)

Written: *Written from 1975 to 1989*. Moscow, 1997. NLO. (Написанное с 1975 по 1989. Москва, 1997. Новое литературное обозрение.)

Written2: *Written from 1990 to 1994. Moscow, 1998*. NLO. (Написанное с 1990 по 1994. Москва, 1998. Новое литературное обозрение.)

Calculations: *Calculations and Findings: Stratification and Conversion Texts.* Moscow, 2001. NLO. (Исчисления и Установления: Стратификационные и конвертационные тексты. Москва, 2001. Новое литературное обозрение.)

Moscow: *Moscow: Verse for Every Day.* Moscow, 2014. NLO. (Москва: Вирши на каждый день. Москва, 2014, Новое литературное обозрение.)

COMMENTARY

UNDER ME (1994)

Text from *Written2*: pp. 245–252 (also in *Calculations*)

In Russian, the title, *pri mne* [при мне], can mean "facing me" or "near me," but while usually a spatial marker, the particle *pri-* also has a temporal sense, used in phrases such as *pri Staline* [при Сталине] or "during Stalinism / under Stalin," "during Stalin's reign." That is, *pri* X denotes proximity to the speaker, either in space or time. A more mundane translation might be "in my time" but *pri mne* is not the common, expected way to say that in Russian. *Pri mne* has a sort of grandeur that "in my time" lacks.

To footnote every proper noun in this work would be to write a concise history of the second half of the twentieth century. That said, the broad sweep of the poem begins with Soviet and other Cold War political figures, from Stalin to two presidents of Finland (Juho Paasikivi, 1870–1956, and Urho Kekkonen, 1900–1986); proceeds to wars and geopolitical changes that would have been covered by the Soviet press; moves on to the great artists who died during Prigov's lifetime, followed by his artistic contemporaries (such as Russian composer Alfred Schnittke 1934–1998), film stars (e.g., Kim Basinger, 1953–present) and athletes (auto racer Michael Schumacher, 1969–present) of his time. He concludes with scientific advances, diseases, global moods, and personal events and figures, steadily narrowing down and simultaneously broadening his focus away from media and propaganda towards the elemental and constant.

DESCRIPTION OF OBJECTS (1979)

Text from *ST*: pp. 90–99

Here Prigov has adapted the rigid jargon of dialectical materialism to descriptions of symbolically charged objects, producing a new Soviet encyclopedia where everything is almost identical to everything else.

OBITUARIES (1980)

Text from *ST*: pp. 138–143

In *Obituaries*, the great figures of Russian literature are memorialized with the canned formulae of the Soviet press, as used in recording the deaths of important Communist Party functionaries. In addition to satirizing the official Soviet verdicts on the giants of Russian literature, it also serves as a bleak comment on the late Brezhnev "period of stagnation," when the USSR was ruled by gerontocrats.

at the age of 38—Pushkin, in fact, died before his thirty-eighth birthday.

mirror of the Russian Revolution—an essay by Lenin praising Tolstoy.

APOTHEOSIS OF THE OFFISSA (1975–80)
Text from *ST:* pp. 149–165/*EPS:* pp 143–171

Offissa—What I have translated as "Offissa" is the Russian *militsaner* [милцанер], a slangy, abbreviated form of the word *militsianer* [милцианер], literally "militiaman," which in Soviet Russia was the normal term for a policeman. *Militsaner*, missing one vowel, is a clipped Moscow way of calling the cop on the beat. Prigov, in his performances of these poems, would heavily emphasize the abbreviation. Having thought long and hard how best to translate the term (Fuzz? Cop? or simply P'liceman, as others have?) I have ultimately chosen, in homage to the seminal American comic book character *Krazy Kat*, to use the term "Offissa"—as in the character Offissa Pup. Like *militsaner*, "offissa" is a deformation of pronunciation, somewhat class-marked. My hope is that this translation relays the cartoonish aspects of public order which are important to Prigov's sequence of poems.

Vnukovo—an airport on the outskirts of Moscow.

Lilienkron—German lyric poet and novelist Friedric Lilienkron (1844–1909).

Oka—a large river in Russia, tributary of the Volga. The Moscow River, in turn, is a tributary of the Oka.

COMPLETE AND FINAL VICTORY (1982)
Text from *ST:* pp. 222–231

Kaluga—an *oblast'* (administrative district) southwest of Moscow; the Oka river runs through it.

Vassily—Stalin's son Vassily served in the Soviet Air Force during World War II and was rapidly and repeatedly promoted, up to the rank of Major-General. After Stalin's death he was imprisoned as a politically dangerous person, and eventually released in 1960.

Jaruzelski—Russian resistance to Polish invasion is an important theme in Russian nationalism. Here Prigov is identifying early 1980s developments in Poland, such as the rise of Solidarity and the imposition (in response to Soviet prodding) of a military government under Jaruzelski, with the Polish invasion during the early seventeenth century "Time of Troubles" following the end of the Rurik dynasty.

HOUSEKEEPING (1975–1986)

Text from *Written*: pp. 5–34

In this cycle, perhaps Prigov's best-known (along with the "Offissa" poems), Prigov offers a series of lyric personae embodying the mundane joys and indignities of late-Soviet public and private life, from long lines for groceries to dishes and laundry at home. Significantly, the speakers often imbue these snippets of the daily grind with lofty philosophical significance, in keeping with the demands of Soviet high culture.

Garden Ring—the ring road in Moscow that is closest to the center.

Nogino—now the Kitai-gorod metro stop, formerly named for Old Bolshevik Viktor Nogin (1878–1924). What is now called Slavianskaya Square was formerly Nogina Square.

"A woman kicked me on the subway..."—one of Prigov's best known poems, appeared in two sequences during his lifetime; in "Terrorism With a Human Face," where we have placed it (on page 90), and in the "Housekeeping" sequence, between "I noticed how hard people sleep in the metro," and "What a slender graceful little mom" on page 78, where we have omitted it.

"Our life comes to an end..."—This poem also appears in the "Terrorism With a Human Face" sequence, where it would come between "The Americans have launched into space..." and "People start off white at first..." on page 91.

TERRORISM WITH A HUMAN FACE (1981)

Text from *ST:* pp. 77–87

Truth and truth—Russian has two words for truth: *istina* [истина] and *pravda* [правда]. Scholar Svetlana Boym, in her book *Common Places* (Harvard University Press, 1995), describes the distinction thus: *pravda* evokes justice, fairness, and righteousness; *istina* derives from the verb "to be" [есть] and means a kind of truth and faithfulness to being. In the Russian Orthodox saying, *"pravda* comes from heaven, *istina* comes from the earth," but the two terms often reverse their meaning. By the nineteenth century, *pravda* is the more colloquial term, while *istina* carries literary and liturgical associations.

Kneeling at the entrance to the tomb—the first poem is a cento composed of lines from a poem by Fyodor Tyutchev (1803–1873), "Nature is not what you think," as well as lines from Robert Burns.

"A woman kicked me on the subway..."—This poem was also included in the "Housekeeping" sequence, where it would have appeared on page 78 in the present edition.

All are Jews—a reference to poet Marina Tsvetaeva's (1892–1941) well-known statement that this was the case with poets.

Spartak, Dynamo—two leading Soviet soccer teams. Initially, Dynamo was affiliated with the police, while Spartak was affiliated with the trade union organization.

"Our life comes to an end..."—Prigov included a poem in this sequence which he also included, with negligible variations, in the "Housekeeping" sequence (see page 84). We have omitted it in "Terrorism With a Human Face" where it would have appeared on page 91, between "The Americans have launched into space..." and "People start off white at first...".

MOSCOW AND THE MUSCOVITES (1982)
Text from *ST:* pp. 178–191

Ashburnipal (685 BCE–626 BCE)—the last strong king of the Assyrian Empire. He assembled a large library of cuneiform documents, which survived and are now in the British Museum. He is often identified with an Assyrian King known to the Romans as Sardanapalus. Sardanapalus supposedly "equated the good life with a life of brute pleasure," and his decadence became a theme in Romantic literature and art, e.g., as the subject of a play by Byron and a painting by Delacroix.

Pyotr Bagration (1765–1812)—Russian General (of Georgian ethnicity), hero of the Battle of Borodino, at which he was mortally wounded. The battle, a tactical victory for Napoleon, nonetheless led to his strategic defeat. A key figure in Tolstoy's *War and Peace*, Bagration is a Russian national hero.

Drang nach Osten—"Push to the East," referring to German expansion into Slavic lands. (Prigov has it in Cyrillic transliteration.)

"Like Rome..."—a Russian Nationalist trope for Moscow as the center of the world empire. The first Rome was Rome itself, the second was Byzantium, and third is Moscow—and there will be none further.

Groys, Kosolapov, Shilkovsky, the Gerlovins, Sokov, Roginsky—late Soviet "nonconformist" or dissident artists, colleagues of Prigov, all of whom emigrated to the west in the late 1970s and early 1980s. Boris Groys is the art critic and philosopher credited with naming the Moscow Conceptualist school, of which Prigov is a major representative. At the time this parody of Soviet anti-dissident rhetoric was written, Prigov had not lived outside the USSR, although later in his life he lived for some time in Germany and traveled internationally.

Erechtheion—ancient Greek temple on the north side of the Acropolis, dedicated to Athena and the sea-god Poseidon.

Akhenaten—Egyptian pharaoh (died circa 1335 BCE) who introduced a monotheistic form of sun worship. (See Freud's *Moses and Monotheism*.) Nefertiti was his queen.

THE IMAGE OF REAGAN IN SOVIET LITERATURE (1983)
Text from *ST:* pp. 244–263 / *EPS* pp. 172–204

Anatoly Karpov—Russian chess grandmaster, world champion at various times. In 1975 he took over the world champion title from the US grandmaster Bobby Fischer, but without actually playing him; unable to agree on terms for the match, Fischer was deemed to have forfeited his title.

Karatsyupa—According to his obituary in the Washington Post of November 23, 1993, Nikita Karatsyupa was a legendary Soviet border guard, hailed by Stalin's propaganda machine as a bulwark against spies and "enemies of the state." Soviet schoolchildren were raised on tales of his heroism, enterprise and bravery. A popular image showed Karatsyupa together with his faithful dog Ingus.

Tsushima—The battle of Tsushima Straits was a major Russian naval defeat in the Russo-Japanese War (1904–1905); on May 27, 1905, the Imperial Russian Baltic Fleet, which had sailed around the world to confront the Japanese, was almost entirely destroyed.

Varyag—At the start of the Russo-Japanese war, the imperial Russian naval vessel, Varyag fought an unequal battle with a squadron of Japanese warships in an attempt to break out from Incheon harbor. Outgunned, the crew scuttled the ship rather than surrender. The name of the ship comes from the Russian word for the Varangians, Viking raiders who are credited with establishing the first "Russian state," Kievan Rus, around the first millennium.

Borodino—site of a historic battle. See note to "Moscow and the Muscovites."

Kulikovo—the place of a battle, in 1380, between ancient Russian principalities and the Mongol Golden Horde. It is generally seen as the turning point in Russia's struggle to lift "the Tartar yoke."

Kliment Voroshilov (1881–1969)—Russian general and defense minister. Although not very competent (he was Defense Minister at the start of the German invasion in 1941) he was a favorite of Stalin.

Lavrentia Beria (1899–1953)—a Stalin-era leader, head of the NKVD (forerunner of the KGB) and in charge of the Soviet atomic bomb program. After Stalin's death, he fell from power and was eventually executed.

Shota Rustaveli—twelfth-century Georgian poet, author of the Georgian national epic, *The Knight in Panther Skin.*

Stenka Razin (c. 1630–1671)—Cossack leader who led a major uprising against Tsarist Russia. He is also the subject of symphonic poem by Alexander Glazunov, in which Razin, surrounded by Tsarist forces, throws his Persian Princess mistress into the Volga, declaring "never have I sacrificed to the Volga, but today I offer it what is for me the most precious of all treasures."

Young Maxim—Maxim Shostakovich, a musician, the son of composer Dmitri Shostakovich. In 1981 he defected to West Germany. His father's Fifth Symphony, "The Leningrad," composed during World War II, was considered symbolic of Russian resistance to German invasion.

Mikhail Kutuzov (1735–1813)—imperial Russian General, hero of wars with Turkey and Napoleon.

Viktor Korchnoi (1935–2016)—Soviet chess grandmaster. He defected to the Netherlands in 1974, and was repeatedly defeated by Anatoly Karpov (see note above).

"his own little son"—Peter the Great had his son, the Tsarevich Alexei, condemned to death for plotting against him.

Pavlik Morozov—a Stalinist martyr-hero, he was said to have informed on his parents to the secret police as traitors. His parents killed him, and were themselves later executed. While probably not an accurate depiction of whatever may have happened, the story was a key element of Stalinist propaganda.

Yekaterina Furtseva (1910–1974)—one of the most important and influential women in Soviet politics. Initially an ally of Khrushchev, she was a Politburo member and a very powerful Minister of Culture from 1960 until her death in 1974.

Akutagawa, *Rashomon*—Akutagawa Ryonosuke (1892–1927), Japanese fiction writer. *Rashomon*, a story told and retold from several perspectives, was made into an internationally successful Japanese movie in the 1950s.

Hisena Habre—dictator in Chad between 1982 and 1990.

Goukoni Oueddei—Habre's rival in Chadian politics and head of state from 1979 to 1982.

OPEN LETTER (1984)
Text from *ST:* pp. 266–271

Brahmins, Sudras—Brahmins are the highest, and Sudras the lowest, of the four traditional Indian castes.

Nikon—seventh Patriarch of the Russian Orthodox Church (1605–1681), whose reforms of the Church led to the schism with the "Old Believer" sect.

Pomor—an ethnic group living in the far north of Russia, on the shores of the White Sea.

Sorokin, Nekrasov, etc.—The biographies of various Moscow Conceptualist artists and writers given here are purely fictional.

TWENTY STORIES ABOUT STALIN
Text from *Moscow*: pp 693–5

This text plays with the late-Soviet received image of Stalin.

Grand Duke Constantine—There were several of this name and title in the Romanov dynasty. This reference appears to conflict Grand Duke Constantine Pavlovich (1779–1831), presumptive heir to Alexander I, who secretly renounced his claim to the throne, with Grand Duke Michael Alexandrovich, who was designated as Tsar after the abdication of Nicholas II in 1917, although he never actually took power, having deferred to the Duma, and was eventually executed by the Bolsheviks.

Anka the Machine-Gun Girl—Russian civil-war-era character in Russian jokes. In the early Soviet popular film *Chapaev*, romance comes from the love between the hero's adjutant Petka and Anka the Machine-Gun Girl.

Leon Trotsky (1879–1940)—Russian revolutionary and chief rival of Stalin, assassinated in 1940 while exiled in Mexico.

Gregory Zinoviev (1883–1936)—Soviet politician, head of the Cominern. A rival of Stalin, he was executed at the start of the Great Purge in 1936.

Nikolai Bukharin (1888–1938)—Soviet politician, leading theorist, initially an ally of Stalin, executed in the Great Purge.

Semyon Budenny (1883–1973)—Soviet General, hero of the Civil War and ally of Stalin.

Karl Radek (1885–1939)—an Old Bolshevik, later in opposition to Stalin. Sentenced to prison during the purges, where he died.

Voroshilov—see note to "Image of Reagan."

Andrei Zhdanov (1896–1948—Soviet politician, ally of (and possible successor to) Stalin. Leader in cultural policy and identified with purges and campaigns against leading Soviet writers and musicians. His death was used as a pretext for Stalin's final terror campaign, "the Doctors' plot," which targeted Jews and "cosmopolitans."

SEVEN NEW STORIES ABOUT STALIN

Text from *EPS*: pp. 240–242

Under Gorbachev, the Soviet Union embarked on a heady round of historical revisionism. In this piece, Prigov gives the post-perestroika image of Stalin the same treatment he gave the older version in the previous poem. Stalin remains a monumental figure, but is now a perfect sneak, cheat, and villain, instead of the wise father of the people.

THE CAPTIVATING STAR OF RUSSIAN POETRY

Text from *EPS*: pp. 243–252

The title of this story comes from a line in Pushkin's poem "To Chaadaev," and probably also alludes to a Soviet "costume drama" film of 1975, about the wives of the Decembrists (unsuccessful liberal revolutionaries in the early nineteenth century) and their decisions to follow their husbands into Siberian exile. The story plays with the facts of Pushkin's life, confusing heroes and villains, and importing anachronisms like there was no tomorrow. For example, the description of Heeckeren's nephew—small, swarthy as a monkey, with a face recalling "either a Negro or a Jew"—corresponds to contemporary descriptions of Pushkin.

George-Charles de Heeckeren d'Anthès (1812–1895)—French military officer and politician, who fatally wounded Pushkin in an 1837 duel prompted by d'Anthès' involvement with Pushkin's wife.

Pyotr Chaadaev (1794–1856)—philosopher, westernizer, and friend of Pushkin.

Gregory Potemkin (1739–1791)—military and political figure, favorite of Catherine the Great. His appearance, along with the (unnamed) Empress, is one of many anachronisms in the story.

Wilhelm Kuchelbecker (1797–1846)—poet, exiled to Siberia for his part in the 1825 Decembrist uprising. His most famous work is an elegy to Pushkin.

Yevgeny Baratynsky (1800–1844)—poet, friend of Pushkin, who had high praise for his writing.

Vissarion Belinsky (1811–1844)—editor, literary critic, and westernizing liberal.

Aleksey Arakcheev (1769–1834)—military and political figure; his name became synonymous with military dictatorship. He was out of power during Pushkin's career.

Vasily Zhukovsky (1783–1852)—poet and literary translator, credited with introducing the Romantic movement into Russia. Of the generation previous to Pushkin, Zhukovsky used his position at the court (as tutor to the Tsar's heir) to aid and protect liberals.

Pyotr Vyazemsky (1792–1878)—poet and close friend of Pushkin.

Nikolai Chernyshevsky (1828–1889)—philosopher, editor, activist, and Utopian socialist, and seminal figure in Russian populism. His 1863 novel *What is to be Done?*, written while in prison, was enormously influential among later Russian revolutionaries, including Lenin.

Nicholas—Tsar Nicholas I (1796–1855; reigned 1825–1855). Competent, dictatorial, and reactionary, suppressor of the Decembrist uprising, Nicholas took a personal interest in Pushkin, acting as his censor and otherwise supervising his activities.

Alexander von Benckendorff (1781–1844)—military general and political figure, founder of the "Third Section," the secret police under Nicholas I, which was also responsible for censorship and surveillance of intellectual and literary circles. He was directly involved in setting the stage for Pushkin's fatal duel with d'Anthès.

Ivan Turgenev (1818–1863)—novelist, leading figure of the literary generation after Pushkin. A realist, *Fathers and Sons* is his most famous work.

Fyodor Tyutchev (1803–1873)—poet and diplomat. Although now considered among the leading Russian poets of the nineteenth century, he was more widely read after his death, having been "rediscovered" posthumously by the Russian Symbolists.

Chornaya Rechka—"Black River," the site where Pushkin did in fact fight his fatal duel with d'Anthès.

Poklonnaya Hill—literally, "Worshipful Submission" Hill, the highest point in Moscow, on the west side of the city.

AND DEAD FELL THE ENEMIES
Text from *EPS*: pp. 253–257

This tale, a kind of hagiography of a Soviet writer, purposefully confuses the lives of Leo Tolstoy and Maxim Gorky, turning them into a single, heroic, patriotic, revolutionary figure. Here, as elsewhere, Prigov gives us the ridiculous, Platonic ideal of "the writer," which he has distilled from the Soviet official culture visions of particular persons. This simplifying, essentializing process is a favorite practice of Prigov.

Yasnaya Polyana—Leo Tolstoy's country estate.

petrel—"The Stormy Petrel" is a revolutionary poem by Maxim Gorky.

The people...were defeated—This refers to the abortive Russian revolution in 1905, which led to some reforms of the Tsarist system.

Capri—From 1906 to 1913, exiled from Russia, Gorky lived on the Italian island of Capri. He had a second period of exile in Sorrento, Italy, from 1921 to 1930, when he returned to the USSR at Stalin's personal invitation.

Rurik—ninth-century chieftain, founder of the Rurik dynasty which ruled first Kievan Rus, then Moscovy, and finally the Russian Empire, until its collapse in the seventeenth century.

Ivan the Terrible—Ivan IV (1530–1584), first Tsar of Russia. (Prior to his reign, the territory was the Grand Duchy of Moscovy.) His sobriquet might also be translated as "Ivan the Awesome." He broke free of "the Tartar yoke" and began the conquest of Siberia.

Third Department—tsarist-era secret police.

THE DELEGATE FROM VASILEVSKY ISLAND
Text from *EPS*: pp. 258–262

Vasilyevsky Island—a district in Leningrad/St. Petersburg.

Martov and Plekhanov—Russian revolutionaries. Julius Martov (1873–1923) was the leader of the Menshevik Faction (Lenin led the Bolsheviks). In Russian, Bolshevik means "majority," and Menshevik means "minority," so Lenin's question refers to the split into factions of the Russian Social-Democratic Labor Party at the Second Party Congress in 1903. Marxist theoretician Georgy Plekhanov (1856–1918) was another prominent Menshevik.

Nadezhda Krupskaya (1869–1939)—Lenin's wife. As Lenin's widow, Krupskaya was a powerful figure in the culture wars of the 1920s, though with a somewhat restricted political role in the 1930s.

Shushenskoe—Siberian town where Lenin was exiled from 1897 to 1900.

Three sons—Lenin and Krupskaya were childless.

FOREVER LIVING
Text from *EPS*: pp. 263–269

June 22—on this day in 1941, Germany invaded the Soviet Union, naturally from the west rather than the east.

Serge Lazo (1894–1920)—Bolshevik leader in the Russian Far East during the 1917 Revolution and the civil war. In 1920, in Siberia, he was arrested by Japanese troops as part of the Allied Intervention (primarily U.S., British, and Japanese troops) in the civil war. It is widely believed that either Japanese or White Forces burned him alive in the furnace of a locomotive on the Trans-Siberian Railroad; the station where it presumably happened is now named for Lazo.

Chinese trader from Kitai-gorod—Kitai-gorod is an older section of Moscow, not far from the Kremlin. The word can easily be understood as meaning "Chinatown" (*Kitai*=China; *gorod*=city), although the name actually refers to a wall built with a particular brick called *kitai* that surrounded the district during the early days of Moscow's expansion.

Life flickers in his copper gaze—Daniil Kharms (1905–1942) uses the unusual locution "copper gaze" in a short story of the 1930s. It's not clear that Prigov would be referring to it, but it would be something he may have been familiar with, as Kharms's work was being circulated in samizdat (underground) publications in his artistic circles. Copper [mednyj] is the common epithet for the equestrian monument to Peter the Great in Petersburg, which features prominently in Pushkin's well-known narrative poem commonly translated as "The Bronze Horseman."

BATTLE ACROSS THE OCEAN
Text from *EPS*: pp. 270–276

In 1980, at the Lake Placid Winter Olympics, the U.S. team defeated the then-champion Soviet team for the Gold Medal. In the US, this was known as "the miracle on ice."

Komsomol—Communist Youth League.

Comrade Shelepin—Alexander Nikolayevich Shelepin (1918–1994), a Soviet politician and security and intelligence officer, and long-time member of the Central Committee of the Communist Party of the Soviet Union. Shelepin belonged to the hard-line faction within the Party which pushed out Nikita Khrushchev in 1964. An opponent of the foreign policy of détente, Shelepin is considered to have been a contender for Soviet leadership, though he was overtaken by Leonid Brezhnev.

AWESOME STONE AVENGER
Text from *EPS*: pp. 277–281

Yevgeny Vuchetich (1908–1974)—Soviet sculptor and artist, known for heroic, allegorical monuments. He was responsible for, among others, the Soviet War Memorial in Berlin and a statue in the United Nations garden in New York, as well as numerous public monuments across the former Soviet Union. Prigov was trained as a sculptor; whether or not he was student of Vuchetich, his initial artistic training would have been in Vuchetich's heroic Stalinist style.

Malakoff—the Malakoff Mound is actually in Sebastopol, not Stalingrad. A sacred site in Russian patriotism, there were important battles there in both the Crimean War and World War II.

monument—Vuchetich's actual Stalingrad monument is in fact an allegorical figure of

Mother Russia holding a sword aloft. At 279 feet, it is among the tallest sculptures in the world.

THE TALE OF ALEXEYEV, THRICE HERO OF THE SOVIET UNION

Text from *EPS*: pp. 282–287

Alexeyev—a common Russian surname; there were at least nine different Heroes of the Soviet Union (a formal decoration) with this surname. I have not been able to determine which might have been the original for this story, which may have been Prigov's intent, as the surname is a common one.

Nanai—ethnic group in the Russian Far East, also known as Goldi or Samagir; linguistically and culturally related to the Manchu.

Karl Marx Stadt—the name of the town of Chemnitz in southern East Germany from 1952 to 1990. When Prigov wrote this piece, the name had not yet reverted.

Little bronze girl—This is a description of Vuchetich's war memorial in Berlin.

MY RUSSIA (1990)

Text from *Written2*: pp. 22–38

"My Pushkin"—a sub-genre of Russian literature, in which the writer explains what Pushkin means to them artistically and personally. Andrei Sinyavsky's *Strolls with Pushkin*, well-known in dissident circles, is a good example from the late Soviet period. Marina Tsvetaeva's *My Pushkin* is another example from earlier in the twentieth century.

Orlov—a town in central Russia, between Perm and Nizhni Novgorod.

Narzan water—a premium brand of bottled mineral water, famous since before the revolution.

Sarmatians—Iranian-origin ethnic group in southern Russia during classical antiquity.

Frederich Schelling (1775–1854)—German idealist philosopher.

Syktyvkar—a town in the northeast of Russia, capital of the Komi Republic of the Russian Federation.

Kolyma—In the arctic Russian Far East, this region was a major node in the Russian prison camp system. Moscow is thus imagined as the capital of the gulag.

EQUILIBRIUM (1997)
Text from *Calculations*: pp. 14–15

Verbilki—suburb to the north of Moscow, famous for porcelain.

Saransk—capital of the Mordovian Republic of the Russian Federation; located in Southwest Russia, in the Volga Basin.

UNBELIEVABLE STORIES (1998)
Text from *Calculations*: pp. 38–40

For some time after the collapse of the Soviet Union, the media was free to print anything that would sell, the more bizarre the better. These little stories invert the sensational fictions offered, with an emphasis on the unpalatable and unavoidable fact of death.

BRAIN POWER (1998)
Text from *Calculations*: pp. 40–41

In addition to Tolstoy, Chekhov, and Dostoevsky, there are Russian writers listed here that may be less well-known to our readers. Short biographies are provided below.

Ignatii Potapenko (1856–1929)—Ukrainian writer best known for *Diary of a Russian Priest*.

Alexander Kuprin (1870–1938)—known mostly as a short-story writer, his representative work is *The Duel*.

Ivan Bunin (1870–1953)—exile writer who won the Nobel Prize for Literature in 1933.

Aleksei Remizov (1877–1957)—a Symbolist who wrote in exile after the revolution.

Yevgeny Zamyatin (1884–1937)—author of the early-Soviet-era dystopian novel *We*.

Mikhail Bulgakov (1891–1940)—successful author and playwright in his lifetime; published posthumously, his novel *The Master and Margarita* is considered among the masterpieces of twentieth-century literature.

Mikhail Sholokhov (1905–1984)—won the Nobel Prize for Literature in 1965; *And Quiet Flows the Don* is his most famous work.

Konstantin Vaginov (1899–1934)—avant-garde poet and author of three novels; associated in the 1920s with the OBERIU group (Daniil Kharms, Alexander Vvedensky, etc.), and several other Leningrad literary circles, including the salons of Mikhail Kuzmin and Mikhail Bakhtin.

Leonid Dobychin (1894–1936)—a fiction writer who came under heavy criticism for "formalism" during the purges and is believed to have committed suicide as a consequence.

Andrei Platonov (1899–1951)—author of *The Foundation Pit* and numerous other works; although frequently criticized for political and aesthetic errors, he managed to survive the purges.

Vladimir Sorokin (b. 1955)—friend and younger contemporary of Prigov; also came out of the unofficial, "non-conformist" artistic world, and had considerable popular success during perestroika and after the collapse of the USSR.

NON-SPURIOUS TRANSFORMATIONS (1998)
Text from *Calculations*: pp. 43–45

Prigov starts from what seems a game to play with a small child, and turns it into an exuberant meditation on the mutability of everything, concluding with the Spirit, asking whether it too can disappear.

nirgunam—from the Bhagavad Gita, meaning "beyond materiality," one of the possible paths to enlightenment, but a very difficult one, because one must give up all attachment to one's senses.

RECALCULATING TIME (1997)
Text from *Calculations*: pp. 101–105

Around the end of the last century, Prigov began to count and multiply and otherwise arithmetize the world around him. Works like this one are built around these metaphysical "back of the envelope" calculations.

VERDICTS (1998)
Text from *Calculations*: pp. 110–112

In this piece, Prigov imagines typical Soviet era crimes and verdicts applied to the animal kingdom and the natural world.

LETTERS (1997)
Text from *Calculations*: pp. 134–136

This poem encompasses an acrostic of the Russian word for the Gospel: Евангелие. In my translation I substitute, letter by letter, the term Evangelion, so the last two letters are by necessity pronounced as one.

RUSSIA AND DEATH (1997)
Text from *Calculations*: pp. 146–148

my own self: 7—The number 7 in Russian is sem' (семь) a near pun to сам, the emphatic pronoun for the self (i.e., myself, yourself, himself). Perhaps also relevant is that the seven of spades card plays an important role in the hero's downfall in Tchaikovsky's opera (based on Pushkin's story) *Queen of Spades*.

Belyaevo—working class region of southwest Moscow, around the Belyaevo metro stop, where Prigov lived for many years up until his death.

ь—the twenty-ninth letter of the Cyrillic alphabet, referred to as the "soft sign," which indicates that the preceding consonant should be softened or palatalized.

THREE SOURCES (1998)
Text from *Calculations*: pp.158–159

Another version includes this final strophe: "There are three sources of everything: something present that animates from within, something external that inspires, accompanies, resists, confirms, or permits itself to be conquered. And in addition, something unexpected, arrived from another dimension, for example."

ABOUT EMPTINESS (1999)
Text from *Calculations*: pp. 185–187

Prigov's version of a Socratic dialogue, this work could also be a theater piece, with the respondent miming some answers.

THE BATHERS (1996)
Text from *Calculations*: pp. 305–308

Chapayevites—Vasily Chapayev (1887–1919), was a famous Red Army soldier and the hero of an important early Soviet film. The Chapayevites came to symbolize the ideals of the Red Army; the name was used for military units and weaponry during WWII.

Simeon of Polotsk (1629–1680)—Belorussian cleric and writer and an important figure in the development of Russian literature.

hesychasts—Russian Orthodox mystics, devotees of uninterrupted prayer. J.D. Salinger gives a good description of their beliefs in his novel *Franny and Zoey*.

WHO I WANTED TO KILL AT VARIOUS AGES (1997)

Text from *Calculations*: pp. 280–283

Prigov lists many names that may be unfamiliar to the reader in this text. In one section he lists most of the prominent victims of the Stalin's purges, targets of his campaigns, military adversaries, as well as Stalin's own colleagues and supporters, and a variety of foreign figures (e.g., Batista, Lin Biao, Mobutu) all conventional villains in Soviet propaganda. Another section lists many of his contemporaries, fellow writers and artists, as well as conservative artistic authorities. Below, I've attempted to gloss the names that may be least familiar to an English-language reader.

Ion Antonescu (1882–1946)—Romanian Fascist leader during World War II.

Syngman Rhee (1875–1965)—Korean politician, important anti-Japanese resistance figure and leader of South Korea (the Republic of Korea) during the Korean War.

Batu Khan—thirteenth-century Mongol ruler and founder of the Golden Horde which dominated much of Russia at the time.

Vuchetich—see note to "Awesome Stone Avenger" above.

Serov—Vladimir Aleksandrovich Serov (1910–1968), Socialist Realist painter and academician, President of the USSR Academy of Artists in the 1960s.

Surov—Anatoly Alekseevich Surov (1910–1987), dramatist and theater critic, twice-winner of the Stalin Prize. During Khrushchev's thaw, he was expelled from the Writers Union as an unreconstructed Stalinist.

Joseph Brodsky (1940–1996)—Russian poet, target of official campaign as a "social parasite" and, after serving a prison sentence and other difficulties, exiled to the west in 1972. Awarded the Nobel Prize in literature in 1987. A native of Leningrad, Brodsky's aesthetic was very different from Prigov's, as was his circle of "non-conformist" artists.

Lev Rubinstein—important poet of Moscow Conceptualist circle, a close friend of Prigov.

Vsevolod Nekrasov (1934–2009)—Russian minimalist poet, loosely allied with Prigov and other Moscow Conceptualists. Nekrasov and Prigov quarreled at some point in the 1980s.

Sorokin—see note to "Brain Power" above.

Viktor Anpilov (1945–2018)—Russian politician, leading adversary of Boris Yeltsin's capitalist reforms.

Erofeyev—probably Viktor Vladimirovich Erofeyev, contemporary Russian novelist, and member of the 1990s literary group EPS (Erofeyev, Prigov, Sorokin). But this may also be an allusion to Venedikt Vasilyevich Erofeyev (1938–1990), dissident writer, famous for the prose work *Moscow to the End of the Line* (*Moskva–Petushki*).

The Patriarch—title of the head of the Russian Orthodox Church.

A LIST OF MY OWN DEATHS (1999)

Text from *Calculations*: pp. 268–271

For context, Prigov was born in 1940, and died of a heart attack on the Moscow metro in 2007 at age 66, eight years after writing this work.

LIST OF OBSERVATIONS (1998)

Text from *Calculations*: pp. 286–289

Prigov is visiting a graveyard, walking through and noting the inscriptions on the headstones, and coming to realize that even anyone's memory of the dead is eventually effaced by time.

Grigoriev, that sounds familiar—He probably sounds familiar to Prigov because there was a famous nineteenth century poet of that name, Apollon Grigoriev, but his dates are different (1822–1864).

Dmitri Alexandrovich Prigov (1940–2007) is one of the most important figures in the literary history of the late Soviet and early post-Soviet era, and is considered one of the founders of Moscow Conceptualism. Prigov was a prolific writer, in all genres, as well as an accomplished visual artist. However, almost until the collapse of the Soviet Union, his writing circulated solely in unofficial samizdat editions and overseas publications. In 1986, he was briefly detained in a Soviet psychiatric hospital, but was released after protests from establishment literary figures. With the onset of glasnost and perestroika, he was able to publish and show his visual art in "official" venues, and also exhibited his art outside of Russia. After the collapse of the Soviet Union, his work was acknowledged with several awards, including, in 2002, the Boris Pasternak prize. He acted in films, traveled widely with performances, readings, and exhibits of his work, and often collaborated with younger artists. Prigov died in Moscow of a heart attack in 2007. His collected works, edited by Mark Lipovetsky, are published in Russia by Novoe Literaturnoe Obozrenie.

Simon Schuchat, a retired American diplomat with more than twenty-five years of service, worked on US–Russian affairs at the State Department in Washington, and in the US Embassy in Moscow. His poetry can be found in several rare books, including *Svelte* (published by Richard Hell when Schuchat was 16), *Blue Skies* (Some Of Us Press), *Light and Shadow* (Vehicle Editions), *All Shook Up* (Fido Productions), and *At Baoshan* (Coffee House Press). A native of Washington DC, he attended the University of Chicago and published the journal *Buffalo Stamps* before moving to New York in 1975 and becoming part of the St. Mark's downtown writing scene. Schuchat was also active in small press publishing; he edited the *432 Review* and founded *Caveman*. He taught at Fudan University in Shanghai, and led workshops at the Poetry Project at St. Mark's Church. His translation of Chinese poet Hai Zi's lyric drama *Regicide* was published in Hong Kong.

Ainsley Morse is a scholar, teacher, and translator of Russian and former Yugoslav literatures, with a particular interest in the aesthetic and social peculiarities of Soviet-era unofficial literature, as well as contemporary Russian prose and poetry. Her translation publications include the *Beyond Tula*, by Andrei Egunov-Nikolev (ASP, 2019) and *Kholin 66: Diaries and Poems* by Igor Kholin (translated with Bela Shayevich; UDP, 2017), Vsevolod Nekrasov's *I Live I See* (also with Shayevich; UDP, 2013), and Andrei Sen-Senkov's *Anatomical Theater* (translated with Peter Golub; Zephyr Press, 2013), as well as a collection of essays by the Formalist critic Yuri Tynianov, translated with Phil Redko. Her book *Word Play: Experimental Poetry and Soviet Children's Literature* is forthcoming from Northwestern University Press. She teaches in the Russian Department at Dartmouth College.

The Eastern European Poets Series from Ugly Duckling Presse

The Eastern European Poets Series at Ugly Duckling Presse began in 2002, and has made available to the English-language reader many historically important texts as well as the newest work of emerging poets from Eastern Europe.

Publications of this scope and depth require many hours of volunteer editorial labor and their publication and production relies on grants, donations, and subscriptions. Please consider supporting the series with a tax-deductible donation, or with a lifetime subscription.

Ugly Duckling Presse, founded in 1993, and incorporated in 2003, is a 501(c)(3) nonprofit and registered charity in the State of New York, and a member of the Community of Literary Magazines and Presses (CLMP). We are grateful for the continued support of the New York State Council on the Arts, our individual donors, and our subscribers.

For more information on how to support the publications in this series, as well as our other publishing programs, please visit our website at www.uglyducklingpresse.org.

ИСТОЧНИК УСПЕХОВ

ВАРШАВА, 5. (Соб. корр. «Правды»). «Союз в авангарде братского сотрудничества со с СССР имеет для нашего народа историческое значение», — пишет газета «Трибуна люду».

Дружба принесла обои плоды. Растет взаимное политическое, хозяйственное, научно-техническое и культурное сотрудничество.

Иван ШЕДРОВ.

УДАРЫ ПАТРИОТОВ

АММАН, 5. (ТАСС). В результате операции, проведенной вчера палестинскими партизанами...

...КИ ВМЕСТО РИСА

...5. (Соб. корр. ...«Правды»). Продолжающийся...

КАКОВ ОН, ВЫБОР ДЛЯ КАНАДЦЕВ?

ОТТАВА, 5. (Соб. корр. «Правды»). Продолжающийся...

ОБМАННЫЙ МАНЕВР

БЕСЧИНСТВА НЕОНАЦИСТОВ

ВЕНА, 5. (Соб. корр. «Правды»). Новые факты бесчинств австрийских неонацистов стали известны общественности страны.

Б. АВЕРЧЕНКО.

ГОРНЯКИ СПЛАЧИВАЮТ РЯДЫ

ХЕЛЬСИНКИ, 5. (Соб. корр. «Правды»). Вот уже 27 дней продолжается стачка горняков компании «ЛКАБ» и концерна Северной Швеции.

В ТИСКАХ ГРИПП...

ЛОНДОН, 5. (Соб. корр. «Правды»).

Тиграм—«сохраненную грам...»

О. ОР...